Happy Birthday
Dad!

D1708423

Jon : Chri

Humpback Island

A NOVEL BY

F. Bruce Steadman

HUMPBACK ISLAND

© 1995 BY F. BRUCE STEADMAN

ISBN
0-9648041-0-7

LIBRARY OF CONGRESS CATALOG CARD NUMBER
95-094693

Cover Art Concept by Kent Steadman
Book Design by Kathy Campbell

PRINTED BY GORHAM PRINTING,
ROCHESTER, WASHINGTON 98579

Contents

Preface

Some Gustavus Truths

Situated just sixty miles or so northwest of Juneau, this glacier and sea-bound community is one of the few flat and sunny pieces of land in Southeast, Alaska. A sand and clay peninsula formed by the cutting of glaciers and the strong tidal action of a narrow inlet of the Pacific Ocean, it is a newly created part of the North American mainland and is surrounded appropriately by Glacier Bay National Park.

When I first arrived in Gustavus, Alaska in the late 1970's, public services included one quaint country inn, a typical western styled National Park Service motel and food service, a one-room schoolhouse and a sixteen by twenty-four foot Post Office. There were no home telephones and no public power services. Only one maintained gravel road stretched ten miles from the airport to the Park Headquarters.

In 1980 there were less than 100 registered voters, half of whom lived principally elsewhere. Government was a once yearly volunteer argument in the one-room schoolhouse. Many full-timers refused to recognize the outcome of the annual discussion since the government was indeed unofficial and individual freedom was more important than cooperation. Part-time summer residents had their ideas about how life should go in Gustavus, and the winter folks usually didn't see it the same way. There were no taxes, no zoning requirements, no license plates, no police, and plenty of heated discussions about how things should be. Most of what this informal government found itself discussing was how to stop some larger entity from influ-

i

encing, if not kaboshing, the community's lifestyle. One hundred or so independent-minded folks tried to prevent the National Park Service, Department of Transportation, Forest Service, Federal Aviation Administration, or big business from doing some terrible damage to them.

The people of Gustavus are an interesting mixture of classic Americana. There were escapees from the city, wilderness groupies, park employees, a few fishermen and homesteaders' families whose roots dated back as far as the first or second decade of the twentieth century. Early federal land giveaways brought loggers from the northwest, cattle ranchers, farmers, and fortune seekers. Those that remained to keep their land claims left large chunks of land to their offspring. Hand-me-down skills in frontiers-manship, heavy equipment operation, and seamanship translated into modern earth movers, fishermen, and mechanics who were able to find enough work to get by.

With no building codes, taxes, or zoning requirements, these hearty people lived life without mainstream modern conveniences. Many of the necessary survival skills were learned as the situation required it.

Over the period of ten or so years from the mid-seventies to the late eighties, Gustavus changed beyond anyone's expectations. It now has electricity, telephone, five guest inns, two restaurants, a new school, a dozen fishing charters, a gas station, a fully stocked grocery store, a lumber and hardware store, a library, two fish processing plants, and a real estate office. Dormant old homesteads, once wilderness and open to free roaming, now advertise land sales and no trespassing signs.

The government continues as an informal discussion by Roberts Rules, now several times a year. Development-caused unsafe drinking water, traffic-related dust or road conditions, rights to the state dock, and the closure of Glacier Bay National Park to commercial fishing are some of the prime topics for argument. Regardless, Gustavus perseveres with no police, zoning requirements, or taxes.

The following stories are a consequence of the profound social and ecological change this powerful but tiny little community has had to weather in recent years. One of the most popular cruise ship destinations in the Northwest and to the ultimate degree an outdoor enthusiast's dream, very few visitors set foot on the land or get the time to try to comprehend what being surrounded by a federal park in the middle of "nowhere" can possibly mean. A few miles to the southeast and again to the south, entire mountain ranges are being clear-cut of their pristine old growth forests. Immediately adjacent to this devastation to the east, north, and west, another federal agency, the Park Service, severely limits a normal person's access for whatever issue is most popular. To the southwest, one of the most delicate marine ecosystems in the world is left unchecked by virtually anybody due to arguments between state and federal agencies regarding "who is in charge of what." Amidst these stark political contrasts, a hearty collection of individualists have created an almost picture-perfect society, with a wonderful school, a volunteer government, a volunteer community service network, and virtually no crime. Activities, both work and play, express family-oriented beliefs and a genuine concern for each other's happiness and welfare.

These writings come with many thanks to Eileen Clark, for her wonderful sense of humor and masterful understanding of the English language; Wayne Clark, for letting me use him and stealing parts of his long hours of stories; my children and step child, Emily, McLean and Megan, for putting up with it all. Last, but, as it proved to be extremely important and impossible without, thank you to Lynda Batchelor and Becky Zimmerman for their professional proofreading. A very boisterous thank you to my artist brother, Kent Steadman, and the same to Mary Hervin for their unfailing support. This book is lovingly dedicated to my father, Frank Moedl Steadman, who loved to read and fish and tell stories. Forgive me dad, for my occasional cussing.

To Fairweather Mountains

ALASKA

HUMPBACK ISLAND

PARK HEADQUARTERS

GUSTAVUS AIRPORT

GLACIER BAY NATIONAL PARK

Bartlett Cove

Point Gustavus

DOCK

PARK BOUNDARY

Pleasant Island

HUMPBACK ISLAND

HUMP

Lemesurier Island

ICY STRAITS

Point Adolphus

To Juneau

To Gulf of Alaska

N

Chapter 1

Earthquake

A SMALL BOAT POUNDED ON A BREAKING SEA. RAPID rising northwesterly water crashed violently against the southeaster wind to toss the boat sideways then propel the bow to mid-air. She had fought the hulking halibut for what seemed like a decade, long before the storm had begun to thrash the water. *Slam* went the bow into the surf. *Zing* went the halibut line again. It was hard to stand up. Her hands were bloody from the fight. The water rolled and broke, hurling the boat to' and fro' like a rubber duck in a bath tub.

Through the noise of the engine and the thrash of water came the voice of my small daughter. She said, "Dad, Dad the house is rolling."

The boat continued to toss and roll. On a big wave I turned to check the foredeck. When I turned back to aft, my former wife was gone; no fishing pole, no halibut, no wife.

"Oh, my God!" I strained to shout. I felt my voice fail with the effort.

My daughter's cry became more insistent. She screamed, "*Dad!* Daddy, the house is bouncing!"

I blinked and rubbed my eyes. The boat bounced and rolled on the waves. Or no, as my vision and the light of the morning cleared, she shrieked again, "Dad…Daddy, the house is bouncing!" She stood on the foredeck with pink teddy bear and soft blanket bundled tightly against her jammies. The boat shuddered and rolled. Windows rattled.

For a flash of a moment my eyes drifted to a close. The

former wife, lost overboard in rough seas, flickered back in. I was heartsick with the loss of another two-hundred-dollar halibut rod. My attempts to shout out to sea began to fade again. Another kind of rolling motion rippled and flourished.

"Dad, Mommy's not here."

Brave tears came into focus. The vision of the boat faded with the gradual onslaught of alternate revelations. I became more alert to the possibility that the pilings under my house were on a roller coaster, not thrashing seas. I forced my eyelids to close, then pried them open. "C'mere quick, kid," I said, "Hide here till it's over."

Emmy jumped into the covers and we snuggled together till the shaking ended. Within moments, we drifted back off to a cozy never-never land.

As I recollect now, sometime later that morning, we loaded up the old pickup truck for the weekly trip to the dump. A fifteen minute ride on four miles of bumpy sand road to the core of Gustavus enterprise became a two hour social excursion. Several neighbors signaled for us to stop along the way to ask, "Did you feel the earthquake?'"

I nodded and most likely replied, "Sure as hell did. The house is still standing, though. Is yours?" Before noon I'm certain that every living soul in Gustavus had asked each other the same question at least once. "Did you hear about the quake on the Juneau radio? The newsman said the epicenter was right under this foot here," and so on.

Hours of earthquake chatter later, I stopped the old Ford amidst a carefully scrutinized void of broken glass zone near the hole in the beach used for a dump site. I tossed the week's garbage into the temporary crater used for twenty years. From the corner of my vision I noticed a train of heavy equipment had rolled down the Gustavus dock road. A handful of men dismounted their mechanical critters and made their way to the business end of the aged wood ramp. I wondered if the supply barge could be due to make its seasonal stop.

My curiosity quickened the usual search of the dump for usable household items. An electric toaster cord, a bent tire iron; they would come in handy for some future project. I threw my bounty amidst the clutter of garbage cans and empty gas containers which occupied the rusted bed of our pickup. Trash day was gas day. Which reminded me: I often pondered the design of a Gustavus invention—a combination gas and garbage container. In other words, "empty the trash and fill the gas."

It makes some sense, really. I had found over the years that those who used the most gas also delivered the most trash to our local crater. Over time, the dump landmass had become less abundant and more premium in value while the number of vehicles on unsurfaced and privately maintained roads had seriously increased. In effect, the relationship between gas and garbage became locally empirical if not scientifically feasible.

My daughter woke me from my mental refuse ramblings by turning the ignition key. *Varoom...pop...pop.* The truck lurched forward and died. The sound of the starter drive ground like a dentist drill on a rotten tooth. I ran to extinguish the painful noise. Back in control, while I pounded on the starter with a broken oar, Emmy turned the key again one more time until the engine engaged. I jumped to the driver's seat and jammed our baldish tires over the very broken glass I had carefully avoided moments ago. "Damn." I could hear the glass crunch and break beneath.

"Let's go check on the fuss at the dock, Em," I said. One hundred yards en route, I felt a thumping near my left rear tire.

"Dad, I think we have a broken wheel or something," Emmy said.

"Uh, yes," I agreed.

We parked near the edge of the wooden ramp, ignored the broken ketchup bottle sticking from the sidewall, and scanned the commotion with my hunting binoculars. The dock sits on a gradual sand beach. In order for the face of the dock to get enough deep water to park a boat at both low and high tide, the ramp, built on treated wood pilings, stretches out a good quarter of a mile or so. Four men stood together on the northwest face of the aging dock with their vehicles now parked neatly behind them. There would be no room for my fifth truck on the small dock.

I turned back to my daughter to find her squishing flies on my inner windshield with my best handyman cotton gloves. "Whap, you stupid bug. Take that, you buzzy bee," she went on.

I chuckled at my daughter's fierce attack on the bee but the wounded tire on the now lopsided truck abruptly arrested the comedy. The spare was aboard under the garbage cans. The jack, however, had been borrowed—I couldn't remember who ran off with it or when. The men on the dock were much more amusing than a flat tire, but it dawned on me that at least one of them would have a jack. Again, we were lucky. On any other day, locating a workable jack somewhere in this community would be at least a half-a-day project. Today, every possible jack owner stood before me.

"Just a minute, Emmy. You smash bugs a minute while I go find a jack to fix our truck," I said. "I'm going down the dock and I'll be right back."

"Me too," daughter replied.

Just ten paces into our quarter-mile hike down the long dock ramp, Emmy's undamaged hundred-percent ears perked. She stopped and yanked my hand back. "Wait, Dad. Did you hear that?"

On cue, I stopped.

"There it is again, Dad," she beckoned.

I can't say I heard a thing at first. But I felt it. "Oh, yeah," I replied. We both focused ahead. The wood planks sounded like a bowl of fresh Rice Crispies in milk. A long dangerous "creak" echoed ahead of our position. I remembered the earthquake.

Rumor had it that several of the dock support pilings were rotten to the core. The earthquake could have shaken them completely loose. The old dock, originally constructed during the war, now belonged to the State of Alaska. Ordinarily, only after a good deal of local screaming, would the state think of funding dock repairs, let alone anything else.

On the unloading face of the dock stood four men dressed in overalls. Behind them in a jumble of parking craftsmanship was a dump truck, a backhoe, a large farm tractor, and a road grader or "cat." One man, Dan, the backhoe driver, walked over and pointed a greasy finger out toward Lemesurier Island. The others followed the westerly direction of Dan's finger and rubbed their eyes for a second look. I scanned with the binoculars to the same direction and my mouth dropped full open. There, about equal distance from the western point of Pleasant Island, the southeast point of Lemesurier Island, and the entrance to Glacier Bay National Park at Point Gustavus was a new piece of land. A strange hump protruded out of the waters of Icy Straits trailed by gradual slopes to all sides. It looked like a...

"Dad," the observant daughter said again, "There's a giant humpback whale sitting over there in the middle of our halibut hole."

"Uhh...right in the middle of our hole, by golly," I replied. The dream from the morning flashed back in. I wondered if my lost halibut rod lay on the highest point of the island's hump.

A sound of another slow "craaa...ck" of stressed wood urged my focus back to the end of the dock. Someone had either let a smelly one or the dock was indeed in serious trouble. All of the men raced in unison for their vehicles. We heard the starters of several machines and then another loud "crrr...ack" followed by an even louder "BANG" like the boom of a rifle. The dock was breaking. One creosote beam after the other plunked into the water followed by more loud cracks and pops. The machines were in reverse, but not soon enough, and the polite and orderly driving craftsmanship that had maneuvered our local contractors into the neat configuration we had first observed had obviously been forsaken. The urgent "hrrr...um" of engines, mufflers, squealing tires, and frantic men faded as if falling from the edge of a steep canyon. First, the backhoe and its driver, then the tractor and so on disappeared off the diminishing dock space.

"Dad, where did they go?"

"For a little swim, dear. Better stay here, honey. I'll go check on 'em," I said.

"What about the tire, Dad?" she called.

"Later, hon. I'll be right back."

I advanced up the weakened wood ramp with caution. The dock creaked and moaned. Over the dock's mournful noises, I could hear muffled unmentionable shouting. I knelt down cautiously and leaned over a broken beam to see that each of the four men had pulled themselves out of the water onto some kind of machinery appendage—a bucket, a tractor hood, or the top of a dump truck bed. While they scratched the saltwater and seaweed from their scalps, the cat driver's son, Wilson, who had been fishing from the beach at the time of the cave-in, jumped on a dilapidated motorcycle and sped past me in a flurry of mufflerless smoke towards town.

I wished I had a camera. Tied up in amusement over the predicament, I was more than slow to think that I ought to do something helpful for these men. They could have been seriously hurt. But the boy on the motorcycle had rescue on his mind, and I had a flat tire and a curious daughter past the dilapidated dock's danger zone.

Emmy had edged her way to my position on the broken dock. Again the daughter observed, "You know, Dad, Willie drives too fast."

"Yup," I said.

The four men bantered various complaints about their plight. I interrupted to call down, "Anything I can do for you fellows?"

"Nothing short of a giant flotation device," Jack Jenkins replied. Jack was the owner of the dump truck. He sat spread-eagle on top of the cab of his truck.

I was about to respond when there came a sputtering rumble noise from the beach behind us. A very old, dinosaur-like contraption made its way tediously down the dock road behind me. A rusty crane that appeared as though it had been dropped from the dock at low tide a few times over was towed by an awkward hybrid of the front end of a 1962 Chevy sedan and the ass end of an International flatbed truck. At the helm was Ol' Gus.

Ol' Gus, the uncle of just about everybody in town, had to be the only one in Gustavus who would entertain the notion to rescue the situation. I suspected that the boy, Wilson, had shared only a piece of the true picture. Nonetheless, it was at least enough news to get Ol' Gus out from under the hood of one of his ancient vehicles and plenty of information to challenge his handyman's appetite, not to mention the possibility of adding a notch in the handle of his storyteller's pistol. He had the one crane on the western end of Icy Strait, although the last I heard it actually operated was back in 1974.

One of those rare individuals who didn't have a mean streak in his body, Gus had been raised here, the son of an early homesteader. Years of remote living had resulted in his ability to fix anything, or at least tinker with it for entertainment on a rainy day. The measure of a happy man in Gustavus, Alaska wasn't so much that the project got done or the machine got running, but rather that the time was well passed fiddling with something until it was time to go to bed. Ol' Gus was a very happy man.

It seemed like a week or so before he went by us headed

down what was left of the dock. With all his sideways attention, it was hard to believe he made it all the way to the end. Fish jumped everywhere on both sides of him. He appeared to be trolling for salmon rather than negotiating an archaic crane down a narrow path twenty feet above shallow water. With each "crack" of the dock another fish jumped.

When the amazing machine finally came to a stop, Gus's attention zoomed forward, scanning. He peered downward and broke into a full smile. "So what are you guys doing down there? Huntin' for lead sinkers or takin' a cold bath with your tractors?" He chuckled and then eyed another jumping salmon.

Hard of hearing, it took a considerable sum of shouting back and forth before Gus lowered the boom down to the first of the stranded men. Very slowly, the backhoe and its driver, Dan, lifted from the water. When it was dock-high up but still over water, Ol' Gus stopped everything, dismounted and hollered, "I can't put you up here, it'll cave us all in." He turned and walked back to the crane before Dan had a chance to disagree.

Dan threw up his hands and shook his head. He was fifteen feet above the water, astraddle a backhoe with no reasonable place to go and definitely not in control of the situation. The crane teetered dangerously. Dan peered down and then up to Gus, cupped his hands and screamed as loud as he possibly could, "Gus! Gus, hold on!"

Gus didn't hear a word of Dan's pleading. Again he looked off to the side down Icy Passage to the east where on the water's horizon he spotted an odd seacraft of sorts. It was headed this way.

Gus squinted for a long moment. When he came to life he hollered, "Hold on a minute, boys. By golly, I've got an idea."

As the craft drew closer it became apparent that it was a landing craft, a beachable flat-bottomed barge. In the days before frequent barge service, this landing craft was a regular sight in Gustavus. Captain Gitgo, they called him, was a wheeler and dealer of sorts, and a former fisherman. He had a way of hustling a dollar out of a pile of junk provided it had to be moved from one place to another. For certain, he had arrived at the right place at the right time. Here before him, half sunk in the debris of the dock, were four of the most competent and usually independent men in Gustavus in a rather dependent and precarious situation. Gitgo's craft was empty.

Not with words but with various arm and hand signals only known to loggers and heavy equipment operators, Gus and Captain Gitgo managed to settle on a solution to the crisis. Actually, it was as if they had planned the whole event beforehand. One by one the four men and their soggy contraptions were lifted from the water to the landing craft.

Ol' Gus was a master with his amazing machine. Wheels and belts screeched and sputtered fitfully. When it sounded like the permanent death of the crane was dangerously near, Gus kept it going with a kick, a bang with a wrench or a nudge. He had the dump truck suspended for almost a half an hour at one time while he tightened a loose bolt on a cable connector. At one point during the ordeal Captain Gitgo turned ashen gray when the cable holding the truck slipped a few inches while suspended over his pilothouse. Gus didn't seem to notice. He kept cranking on the nut.

When the four machines and their owners were finally stacked onto the foredeck of Gitgo's craft, everybody smacked their forehead with a greasy open palm at the same time as if someone yawned and the yawn magically caught on.

Emmy nudged me. She looked up with a puzzled expression and said, "It's low tide, Dad. Where are they going to go?"

"Ha! So it is," I replied. Gustavus was, for all practical purposes, high and dry. The Salmon River was not navigable for at least four more hours. The beaches were no more than two feet deep for hundreds of yards. At best, Captain Gitco's craft could only get a few more feet closer to shore than the equipment currently sat and the dock, of course, was out of commission. Four entrepreneurs stood motionless, one hand on brow, one hand in each of their pockets. They peered across the water at Pleasant Island. Nope, no steep, low tide beaches. Again, in unison, the four-way gaze veered over to the new island.

It was Captain Gitgo who noticed the captive audience's gaze towards the hump and proposed the alternative. He had been on a freight run to the fishing community of Pelican, about fifty miles to the west. In the interest of time and a temporary solution, the Captain proposed an exploratory trip and possible temporary landing for the four men and their machines on the new island. It appeared from this distance that the slopes were sufficiently steep at the water's edge on the south side to allow a successful beaching. He would pick them up on the following day for a return to the mainland at high tide.

Jack, the dump truck owner said, "By gosh, guess we got no choice."

The tractor owner, Hank, now atop the dump truck, said, "I'm game. Might as well take this opportunity to have a look-see." Both shook their heads, threw up their hands and nestled into their operator seats for the ride.

With not another word, the freight captain went to work doing what he knew best. He set a course for an unmarked island dead center in his route to his final destination, rescued some old friends and retrieved another dollar.

Following a careful appraisal of the jumping salmon, Gus put his dinosaur in reverse. Ahead of the odd machine, Emmy and I walked the quarter mile back up the ailing dock ramp and went to work on my glass-infested tire. Emmy supervised for a moment or two and then mooched a five dollar bill for an ice cream at the local mercantile. When his contraption got close, Emmy put on her best smile, stuck out her thumb and caught a ride with good Ol' Uncle Gus. Actually, he never stopped. Gus held out his wrinkled hand for her and she jumped aboard.

Several curses and a dozen minor wounds later, the spare allowed me and the pickup back on the road. Willie, the boy on the motorcycle, zoomed past to resume his fishing on the end of the now broken dock.

I found Gus and my daughter on a bench outside the mercantile slurping ice cream bars. Frank the fisherman had joined them to pause for a soda.

Frank was one of several Gustavus residents who referred to themselves as escapees. Having tried other states, cities, marriages, and life-styles, Frank finally opted for the life of a commercial fisherman. In his mid-thirties, he was ruggedly handsome in a babyface sort of way. A few years back he made his last escape from the capital city of Juneau where he skipped out on a government job and went for the fishing life with a small wood handtroller. He worked his way up to a respectable forty-foot power troller and moved to Gustavus to avoid high rent and his last ex-wife.

"Hey there, guys," I greeted. "So what's the next project?"

"No, no, none for me, thank you," Gus answered.

"Dad...I'm not a guy," Emmy insisted.

Frank nodded and took another gulp of his soda.

"Hey, Frank, your box is full of camp food," I observed.

"Yup, I guess it is." He patted an open cardboard box full of packaged rice dishes, candy bars, and instant drinks. "Cindy's got me roped into my first kayak trip this afternoon," Frank replied. "I suppose you all felt the earthquake."

"Yup," Emmy answered, "and did you see the new humpback whale over there?" She pointed a gooey finger out past the broken dock.

"No...no, I sure didn't," Frank replied. He stood up to try to get the height to see where Emmy was pointing. "I'll be damned. There sure is a hunk of land out there in the halibut hole."

"Hey, that's my dad's secret halibut hole," Emily argued. "How did you know about it?"

We all laughed.

Gus smiled and began to explain. "I've been fishing in your secret halibut hole for sixty years is now a hunk of mud and seaweed..." he sputtered with a mouthful of vanilla and chocolate.

I interrupted in order to give Gus a chance to swallow. "It must have jumped out of the Straits during the quake, Frank," I said. "And did you know the dock just caved in?"

"Nope, I didn't. Guess I better get on down to the river and check the boat. See you guys later." Frank stood up, grabbed his groceries and waved us good-bye. He strapped his cardboard box into a homemade basket on his vintage Schwinn bicycle and pedaled in the direction of Emmy's pointing finger.

Chapter 2

The Land Claims

THE STRANGE ISLAND WITH THE HUMP HAD JUST that morning been at the bottom of Icy Strait. As the explorers drew closer to the southeastern shore, it became clear that it was no small island. They could see from their vantage point smooth mud and sand, natural coves, large rock abutments and steep beaches with deep blue waters surrounded their vantage point. Gulls and other seabirds had flocked en mass to the easy food left on land from the sudden upheaval. Crab and other bottom creatures clambered for the water's edge from the now lofty slopes.

Captain Gitgo picked the first deep water beach to unload the curious crew. It didn't take them long to realize they had found something here. The single hump was of mountainous proportions. Canyons from the ocean floor now climbed to 800 feet above the water. Long sand beaches on all sides gave way to rock coves at the base of the cliffs. The hump tailed to two definitive points on the northernmost side. A cove divided the points creating the tail of the humpback. On the southern side was a gradual peninsula with a rocky spine top. At the point of the spine was a fifty-foot cliff to the water.

It was Dan Madden, the backhoe driver, who after towing the dump truck up the beach from the landing craft, vocalized the island's peculiar shape and announced, "You know, guys, we're the first people ever to set foot on this new piece of rock. I hereby name it Humpback Island."

Dan was one lucky guy and a hard worker to boot. Of the

four men, he was the youngest. His father owned the Park Service concession at one time but went bankrupt and had to sell out. Dan had a disability: He couldn't read or write; he was dyslexic. Five years earlier, Dan returned to Gustavus and signed on as crew on a fishing boat. But the owner, a heavy marijuana user, went over his head in debt and lost the boat to creditors. When his father decided to subdivide the Gustavus properties he purchased years before, Dan put up a down payment on a backhoe and contracted with his father to build the roads. Each time a parcel sold, the owner would hire him to clear the building site. One very wealthy parcel owner, an attorney from Los Angeles, happened to have a gorgeous daughter named Megan. Dan, in turn, was extremely handsome and muscular. Soon after Megan and Dan got married, Megan's father up and died, leaving the entire family fortune to the young couple. Dan worked ten to twelve hour days clearing land and building roads even though he didn't need to. They were known to have the biggest house in Gustavus. Many of the annual house parties, such as Christmas and Halloween, were held in their home.

Hank, the tractor driver, was thinking out loud: "Humpback Island, huh. The environmentalists will think it's theirs just because of the name. But I was the first one on this beach. We're the first human beings to set foot on this land. It's got to mean something, don't you think? Hmmm."

Hank had been a banker in Seattle and in his off time an avid outdoorsman. In the early fifties he met a school teacher on summer vacation from teaching in the one-room schoolhouse in Gustavus. She told him great stories of the beautiful Glacier Bay. She talked of lush gardens, fields of wildflowers, and streams teeming with salmon and trout. When she returned to teach in the fall, Hank came with her for a visit. He fell in love with the teacher and the scenery. As a wedding present Hank bought an old one hundred and sixty acre homestead for fifty bucks an acre. Since then, they visit every summer for the gardening and fishing.

"Not a whole lot of road to grade over here," Bert, the grader owner, said. He was busy wiping sand and mud from his expensive machine. "Sure could use some rags and oil. Wonder if the damn thing'll start?" he mused.

Bert Johnson was a strapping man of over six feet in his early fifties. His parents had homesteaded land in Gustavus forty years earlier and left most of it to him. After spending his early youth here, Bert joined the marines to serve in Korea and then went on the road with large construction firms and helped build the Alaska pipeline on the North Slope. He was married once and had two kids twenty years ago. But while on the North Slope, his ex-wife ran off with a vacationing truck driver. Mostly alone, he drank a little, had plenty of money from the recent land boom, and sometimes spent his winters in Hawaii. Bert was known for his kind-heartedness when other neighbors had domestic difficulties. He was the first to offer condolences, a shoulder to cry on, and a mug full of whiskey.

"Better blow out the carburetor and dry off the battery terminals," Jack, the dump truck owner, said. Jack was a younger man. He moved here to work at the Park maintenance shop in 1972. He had a wife, three kids, a dog, and two horses, all who begged him to stay on in Gustavus when it looked like the regional office in Denver wanted to transfer him farther north. He bought a dump truck from the Park Service auction, a chunk of land from Dan's dad, and started a business hauling dirt, sand, and firewood for a good living during the construction boom. His wife and kids sold garden vegetables to the local lodges and cafes. In the off months, Jack fixed just about anything that was broken.

"Humpback Island, eh…," Bert said. "Pretty weird hunk of real estate. Maybe we ought to see what we've found here."

"I heard you say 'real estate,'" Dan commented. He looked

at Bert and thought a moment. "Maybe we stumbled on something here, guys. It could be worth something." The others looked at him incredulously.

"Are you kidding me?" said Jack. "We just got here."

Bert and Hank took the hint and dove for their machines. There were frantic maneuvers under the hoods; air cleaners flew, electrical connections were wiped and blown, starter motors whined relentlessly, and one by one they raced off to claim a piece of the strange new real estate, Humpback Island.

Captain Gitgo watched in disbelief as his customers scattered in a frenzy of sputtering, wet vehicles. Not a one of them took time to say good-bye to the Captain or check the time of his return to pick them up. He shook his head and pulled away from the beach. As he pushed the throttle up to full, only the tractor remained in sight.

The captain picked up the handset of his marine radio and called to shore, "Hey, Gus, you on this one?"

"Yep...yep...sure am," Gus replied.

"All safe and sound over here," the captain drawled into the microphone, something he had said hundreds of times before. "At least when I dropped 'em off they were. Might be some new land feuds by tomorrow. Maybe even a couple of new subdivisions. But then, once the freight is safe ashore, it's not my problem any longer. Over."

"Same ol', same ol'," Gus groaned. "Better get 'em home to work on this dock before there's any shooting. Over."

The captain laughed. "Look for a dock on the new island before the Gustavus dock gets fixed. I'll see ya tomorrow." He clicked the hand microphone down.

"Yep, I better see if I can get this old heap home before it falls in the lake, too. Ought to get my fishing pole out here after lunch," Gus ended. Gus double clicked the speak button on his microphone and squinted at what was left of the dock. His gaze diverted to the jumping fish.

Fog had set in the next morning. Boats and planes were not moving. Out of the mists so common in Icy Strait a lone kayak cut along the swift but smooth tidal current. Two individuals, dressed in red neon float devices and colorful hand made wool caps protruded above the glassy gray water.

"What's that?" a strong female voice announced. "God, I hope it's Gustavus."

"I'll never get into one of these dumb things again. Never!" a gruff male voice interrupted.

"C'mon, Frank...This is your first time. Don't be such an old stick-in-the-mud," the woman said. "You wouldn't even be out of your sleeping bag yet if we were still over on Point Adolphus."

"Bull...shit! We'd be sipping coffee at home if we had an engine. You can take these floating coffin torpedo things and give them to the Parkies to float around in. Permanently!" Frank exclaimed.

"I'll be damned. Cindy, what is that?" Frank asked as he squinted through the fog ahead of the kayak. "There aren't any hills like that by Gustavus," he said.

"Huh...where are we, Pleasant Island?" Cindy wondered.

Frank continued to squint as though he needed glasses. He rubbed his eyes and picked up the pace of his paddle strokes. Without words, they beached their tiny craft below a large fog-obscured landmass. Cindy looked at her compass. Frank searched a few steps up and down the beach.

Cindy broke the silence, "If I read this right, we should be halfway between Point Gustavus and the Goode River."

"No way," Frank replied. "What did you put in your tea this morning? There aren't any hills around Goode River."

Cindy shivered and mumbled, "This is spooky. Kind of like we're in the twilight zone."

"No, no. It's that new earthquake island. You know. The one from yesterday. I'd forgotten all about it. Hold it...Stop!"

Frank whispered. He held his arms out like an umpire calling the runner safe. "I hear something."

Cindy obeyed. The faint clatter of an engine consumed the fog's silence. As the noise came closer, a farm tractor appeared in the mist heading down the beach towards them.

"No, we must be in Gustavus," Cindy argued. "That's old Hank mowing the beach grass again."

Frank relaxed his arms, dropped them to his side with a bang and let out his inhaled breath.

A male voice lifted through the sputter of the wet engine and fog. "Hey, you folks on my beach, no trespassing."

The tractor coasted within a few yards of the lost interlopers and slowed to an idle. Hank, in his usual new brown coveralls, climbed from the tractor and walked towards the dumbfounded couple.

"Where are we, Hank? We didn't plan on trespassing. Confounded kayak here got us off the mark," Frank acknowledged.

Hank flailed his right arm in a sweeping gesture. "This is my new island. Came upon it yesterday afternoon. Must have jumped up during yesterday's earthquake. The boys and I caught a ride over with Captain Gitgo and have decided to file a claim."

"Oh, boy...here we go again," Frank mumbled.

"What's that now?" Cindy asked, turning away with one ear cocked.

The sound of another engine lifted over the hum of the tractor. From the opposite side of the trio came a backhoe. Seaweed dripped from its turned-up front-end scoop. A handsome man in his early thirties sat in the driver's seat. He raised his right hand in greeting. "By golly!" he exclaimed. "Gettin' sort of crowded on this little hunk of sand. Hi, Frank, Cindy. Hank tryin' to scare you off? Ha! Probably tried to deposit your money, too."

"Now, just wait a minute," Hank objected.

"What the hell is this all about, Dan?" Frank asked. "We were just trying to get home in the fog in that useless torpedo thing there, and here we are on this beach that came into existence just a day ago."

"Kind of a nice beach, though," Cindy added. "Hank says he's already filed claim to it."

"I guess that's sort of debatable," Dan argued, looking at Hank with a smile. "After our swim at the dock yesterday, he was the first off of Gitgo's craft. Hank was always pretty quick. But I guess I've confused it all a little by staking out all the property above the tideline on this side of the island. He might have the beach nabbed, but I got him cut off to dry land. By golly, he might get a little wet inside the boots now and again."

"Just a minute, here..." Hank tried again with no luck.

"Yeah, then there's Bert and Jack up on that hump," Dan went on. "I put a few scoops of sand in Jack's dump for traction. Last I saw him, he was pushing a road over the top of the hump with the help of Bert's blade. Bert saw me staking the high ground and said he and Jack had the other side staked out so don't bother."

"Come on, you guys. You can't do this," Cindy responded in an intentional whine. "This poor island is just a day or two old and you already have it divided, developed, and sold. What gives you the right to..."

"Ain't my fault," Dan argued. I'm just trying to watch out for my fishing rights."

"Fishing rights?" Frank was starting to get a bit riled. "According to Hank here, you have to get his permission to step on the beach." How the hell are you going to get on or off the island? For that matter, you're stuck. And as for Hank, hope he doesn't get stuck here in his socks on a high tide. He'd have to get your okay to dry off. Heaven forbid if anybody wants to take a hike to the afternoon sun on the other side of the hump up there. They'd have to talk to Bert and Jack for a permit to watch the sunset."

The fog lifted. The sound of a fully accelerated outboard engine interrupted the discussion.

"Oh, my gawd!" Cindy exclaimed. "Not another...my gawd, it's Ranger Rick and the Park Service whale patrol."

A souped-up Boston Whaler with the blue National Park decal, various hi-tech boating antennas, and a highway patrol speed radar swung forthrightly towards the beach explorers. Standing at the helm was Ranger Rick in green uniform, a World War I Roosevelt hat, and an official smirk on his face. A transplant from Yellowstone last year, he changed from the international bear spleen detail to whale speed zone cop.

Rick Williams, just 27 years old, blond and blue eyed, originally from Colorado, took his job and his uniform seriously. His biggest disappointment on the Alaska tour of duty was the embarrassing fact that most of the humpback whales in the area stayed outside the National Park boundaries. The Park went to lots of trouble creating a hullabaloo over speed zones for whales when the whales preferred the fast action of Icy Straits. Ranger Rick spent a lot of time chasing whale watchers around the Park for no credible reason. It reminded him of stopping motorists for long hair and flower painted vans; something his father once did as a city patrolman in Durango, Colorado during the seventies.

Another disappointment of Rick's had a lot to do with Cindy. You see, Rick believed he was heaven-sent, a divine gift to women. He also had a crush on Cindy, one of the only available women in Gustavus and a dutiful Park Service employee until she ran head-on into Rick. Cindy, being a student of whale behavior and not male misbehavior and government bureaucracy, opted to spend her time on a fishing boat outside the Park's jurisdiction.

Cindy met Frank by joining his employ as an impromptu

crew during a commercial halibut season. During this particular halibut opening, Ranger Rick, accompanied by Cindy, boarded Frank's boat while on a whale count. When the Ranger wrote Frank a warning ticket for doing twelve knots in a ten-knot speed zone, Cindy jumped ship. She tried to reason with Rick about busting poor Frank when not a single whale had been spotted in Glacier Bay in over a month.

Rick was unbending. "It's the law," Rick proclaimed, not wanting to seem weak or arbitrary in the presence of the lady.

"Well, Rick, dumb jerk, this is just nonsense!" Cindy huffed. "Hey skipper, need any help?"

"As a matter of fact, I do," replied Frank.

And that was that.

Rick nosed the Park Service speed craft up to the beach dangerously close to Cindy's kayak. He dismounted and said, "Good day, folks. Don't suppose you got those tractors here with a kayak, now, did ya?"

All four of the explorers stood with their arms crossed and their feet firmly planted in the soft sand. Everyone replied with a blank stare.

The ranger broke the heavy silence. "Well, this is an interesting new geological formation. Suppose you folks are checking it out. Really, how did you get this tractor and that backhoe over here?"

"Landing craft," Hank offered. "Gitgo. He dropped us off and went to Pelican."

"I hope none of you have developed any ideas," Rick replied. "The superintendent has asked for emergency protection for this new formation. It's just outside the Park boundary, and due to its unusual geological origin, we believe the U.S. Department of Interior should move to protect it at the outset. Not to mention it's smack in the middle of the whale waters. On my way from Point Gustavus, I saw six humpback whales, and..."

"Now just a damned minute, here," Frank interrupted.

"Why don't you get in your silly speed boat and...and..." He was about to shove the ranger down the beach when Dan stopped him.

"Hold on, Frank. Don't get excited," Dan said. "The government can't be all that quick. It took them a hundred years to realize Gustavus was even on the planet, then they wanted that, too. Let the ranger amuse himself."

"I already have claim to this beach," Hank added. "Here's all my witnesses. You're going to have to take us all to court if you think the government can just step in and steal this here land from us."

"Yeah," Cindy jumped in. "Get off Hank's beach, Ranger. You're trespassing!"

"Wait a minute, now. This isn't Hank's beach," Frank complained. "As far as I'm concerned, it's nobody's beach. Go be official someplace else, Rick. We'll take care of this."

Just then a large humpback whale breached not more than a hundred yards from them. Its tail hit the water with a giant splash, shocking the audience into a moment of silence.

Cindy ran to fetch her binoculars from the kayak. Rick jumped towards his cruiser to get a better view of the beast.

"Hey, Ranger, don't get too close," Frank yelled. "It's against the law to harass a whale, ya' know."

"Ought to be against the law to harass us locals," Hank added, as Rick pushed the accelerator to full throttle.

"C'mon, Frank, let's trespass a little on nobody's new island," Cindy said. "While there's a debate over ownership, let's check it out."

Hank and Dan watched as Frank and Cindy paddled down the shore. Gitgo's landing craft came into view out of South Pass to the west. The fog had lifted to reveal patchy sun.

Frank struggled with his paddle trying to get the blade at the right angle. "This is the last time, Cindy," Frank said. "Damned kayak! Sneaky little torpedo is probably scaring the whales away. Ought to be a law against 'em. You'd think we were tourists or something. Next thing you know we'll be dropping Nikon cameras on 'em like little bombs from a Japanese attack."

"Just be quiet, Frank," Cindy replied.

Chapter 3

Our New Island Home

As told by Cindy Certain

WE LEFT HANK AND DAN ARGUING ON THE BEACH that morning and paddled all the way around the new island. Later on, we returned to Gustavus to retrieve some more gear. Frank insisted on loading his fishing boat, not my kayak, with a large canvas tent and a few two-by-fours. I said, "Deal, if we can take the kayak along too."

The following day we ventured back to the island to find that Hank, Dan, Bert, and Jack had abandoned their respective projects and returned home to Gustavus.

At the Fence Post, one of our two local cafes, Aunt Bess overheard Hank's wife saying that the boys got into one hell of an argument about the island's ownership. According to Hank's wife, Vera, when the men touched base on the island, Jack tried to tell Hank that the land claim ought to be in all of their names as partners. Hank disagreed and an argument developed. When the name calling got good and colorful, Norm Coskey, the chief ranger, showed up on the scene with Ranger Rick. Norm arrested Jack for threatening bodily harm and evicted the whole bunch of them. Vera said Jack really didn't threaten bodily harm. It was something more like "I wish someone could knock some common sense into your greedy skull."

Then all four men sided together against the long arm of the federal government and jumped all over Norm about the question of his authority outside the Park boundary. Well, no one ever questions Chief Ranger Norm's authority about anything. Norm sent Rick to the boat to call for state trooper assistance on the marine radio.

The troopers arrived from Hoonah two hours later. By then the island was deserted. Since the lawmen had come that far, they toured the island and then ran over to the Park headquarters in Bartlett Cove for a little courtesy visit between police agencies. According to Chief Ranger Norm, the Native state trooper assistant said he believed the island would be declared Native Lands. The assistant quoted some Federal Law about it.

Rumors around have it that all four of the island's explorers slipped away quietly in order to prevent further disaster when Ranger Rick and Chief Ranger Norm got into an argument about who owned the wildlife—humpback whales in particular—outside the federal boundary. Ranger Rick's position was that the U.S. Government owned the whales. Norm believed that nobody in particular owned them because they migrated through international boundaries.

Hank, Jack, Bert, and Dan had decided that they were quite hungry. Captain Gitgo slipped his landing craft up the beach and the boys drove their machines aboard unnoticed by the hot-tempered rangers.

Anyhow, Frank and I ignored the whole circus of events in a show of sensible protest. We found a nice level and sunny location, put up our tent, and set up what turned out to be a lasting camp. You see, we believed that no one individual, agency or tribe really owned the earth anyway, no matter where it was. We thought we could at least erect a temporary shelter for anyone who happened along. I made a sign on the beach that read:

"HUMPBACK ISLAND:
THIS LAND BELONGS TO NOBODY
ENJOY!"

I went about making our tent comfortable. Every now and again, maybe several times each day, I took a break from the tent stuff to conduct some serious whale watching and exploring. The whales were just absolutely incredible. This island seemed to be magic. The whales would swim right up next to the shore. They would breach, jump, and splash within inches from my fingers. You better believe the Park rangers would freak if they knew I could get this close to a whale.

After three days or so, Frank got restless and decided to get the rest of his camping gear—indeed, all his worldly belongings from his little rented one-room cabin in Gustavus. I didn't have much to move other than my pack, sleeping bag, binoculars, and a few personals, so we moved everything into the canvas tent.

I made Frank build an outhouse while I tried to organize. We put a tarp up alongside the tent with driftwood poles for drying clothes and cooking on my campstove. The menu was fish nearly every single night and leftover fish sandwiches made with pilot bread crackers during the day.

A week later, I guess Megan and Dan heard about the tent and sent over a landing craft full of building materials. My god, that was sure nice of them. But with the materials came a note: "We filed a claim on the land over there. But as long as you guys stay on, we think you ought to have a real roof over your heads. You can pay us back in fish."

Frank and I stacked the material above the high tide line and then talked a long time about whether to really use Dan's materials. I felt like he was trying to buy us off. On the other hand, after three weeks the eight-by-ten-foot tent was getting a bit close. Frank and I weren't even an item yet, let alone ready to build a place together. It's one thing to be in close quarters to the skipper of your boat and quite another to share that kind of space on land.

Plus, neither of us had much money, although I still had a little saved from the Park job. Frank had to buy a new diesel engine for his troller this year. The fishing was good and the price of fish was just okay. My crew share was twenty percent, but I missed a lot of fishing time since this crazy island came out of nowhere.

What finally solved our dilemma was a midsummer storm that came out of the southeast and sent the roof of our tent into Icy Straits. Everything got soaked. And Frank was off moving his boat to Gustavus—up the Salmon River—when it started to blow. All alone and wet, I held onto the tarps for dear life.

In the end, not only did we decide to build the Dan-Megan-Cindy-Frank house, Frank decided we had to build a small dock for the boat. When half the town of Gustavus showed up to help with the building, I felt somewhat over-whelmed. Our design for the house was a small two-story with a combined kitchen/living area and two little bedrooms upstairs. But with so much company the plans kept stretching. What resulted was twice the size of what was planned, with three bedrooms to allow for company, a real kitchen with plenty of space for a big dining table, and an actual bathroom. The new cabin looked pretty hilarious sitting out on the beach all by itself surrounded by two dozen red, blue, and green tents.

Some of our friends brought baby trees to plant. Aunt Bess brought several berry bush starts and Ol' Gus sank a well. Dan and Megan brought their own materials and put up another small guest cabin. Jack Jenkins brought his whole family over for the affair, including Willie and his motorcycle, who nobody saw again till the event was over. Willie put a motorcycle track on every square inch of the island's beaches.

Wilbur Cook, the Gustavus school teacher, brought some old school chairs and a dozen duck decoys for "ornamental purposes." When the rolled asphalt roofing was complete as well as the homemade barrel wood stove installed, we gathered drift-wood for a fire and had one very fun potluck. Even Pastor Green from the Gustavus Chapel helped with a blessing of the new house on the new land. "May the future of this island be one of peace and harmony with the universe. And may wicked corporations and evil big governments keep their greedy little thumbs off of it," she prayed.

When it was time for the volunteer crew to leave to cross Icy Strait to the mainland, many promised to return. And, little by little, some of them did. Aunt Bess sent her sons over to build a cabin for her. A fisherman and his wife from Sitka and a patch of kids moved over in their boat. Ol' Gus tinkered for months, bringing boatloads of junk, equipment, and building supplies. He told me one time over a cup of coffee in between boat loads that he preferred the homestead spirit to wild-eyed tourist traps. "By golly," he added, "better to spend time fussin' about livin' than fussin' about gettin' rich." Little by little, so began the settlement of Humpback Island.

Chapter 4

A Better Place

(As told by Fisherman Frank Stellar)

I NEVER EXPECTED TO BE A FOUNDING FATHER OF anything, let alone this strange collection of humankind on a mysterious earthquake island in Icy Straight, Alaska. It was pretty darned peculiar how we got on this island in the first place. If the wind had blown one degree different on that first, and certainly the last, kayak trip from hell, I'd be still fighting tourists for dock space over in Gustavus.

Cindy and I only meant to spend a few nights on the island when we set up the first camp. She was mad at me for being a boob about the kayak. I suggested we go back for a night or two to save face, really. But this time we took the fine old fishing vessel "Buzz Lady," and I didn't have any plan to make either the island or Cindy a permanent arrangement.

Not only is it weird that we should wind up living on this island, it is a bizarre story that led to my living in the middle of "Nowhere-Alaska" in the first place. I wasn't born and raised here; I have no relatives within two thousand miles except Cindy. And you know what? There's only one thing that brought me here—fishing, and there's two things that keep me here—fishing and Cindy.

Okay, I guess there's more to it than that, really, like elbowroom from crazy city people, and I wouldn't trade the notion of being my own boss out on the water with any poor sucker doing eight-to-five with Ms. or Mr. Stick up the ol' you-know-what for a boss. And if I get lonely, there's plenty of good folks to keep you company when you need them. So, yes, I'm planted here. I'll never move unless the Almighty is the mover.

I suppose that I'd still be one of Gustavus' very own yippie-do-strawberries over there if luck hadn't transplanted me ten miles out on this island. I'm happy for that twist of fate now since Gustavus has grown to be more like bigger places. Just like Juneau or Seattle, they have dump problems. You know, the government won't let them dump anything anywhere. The EPA's closed the old dump and the State Division of Lands won't let 'em use any other spot within six thousand miles. You'd think the governor would talk things over with himself. "Hello, hello, this is me, the governor. Ya know, Gov, I have some garbage over here and need a place to put it," and so on.

Then there's road dust. The government spends millions of dollars advertising to bring "yuppie tourists" and "gray-power adventurers" to pristine outback Alaska and then won't spend an extra nickel on the dust the traffic causes. The locals get in fights because the same good intentioned person makes a living from causing the traffic and then badmouths his own customers for kicking up the toxic dust. What are you gon'na do. I call it "tourist pollution."

Cindy made a sign for the outhouse. It says,

"ARE YOU ENJOYING THE DOUBLE BIND?
POOP NOW—PAY LATER.
YOU ARE CURRENTLY CAUSING
ENVIRONMENTAL DAMAGE!
IF YOU LET IT SLIDE, YOUR KIDS
WILL HAVE TO SLIP IN IT."

Ah, yes, and then there's my favorite hassle—boat moorage. The historically safe moorage of Bartlett Cove is off limits to ordinary or local people much of the year. You see, it's in the

only private club in Southeast Alaska—the National Park. I call
it Glacier Bay Club Med. And it's operated by the only elite
class of arrogant-headed yuppies within a five- hundred mile
radius other than the obsessed politicians in Juneau. Department of Interior bureaucrats, bookworm biologists, super environmentalists, and their respective friends and families think
they are the only precious humans worthy of basking in God's
wilderness. Throw into this a well-known, nation-wide, good-
old-boy shady deal with political friends who happen to have a
corner on the Park Service concession contracts. Did you know
our tax dollars allow private profit-making businesses to steal our
money at every rock in a national park? These are the question-
able guys that run the hotels, boats, airplanes, greasy spoons, and
gift shops. These same guys have been able to convince the
National Park Service that it would conflict with their business
to have ordinary people park their boats in the one and only safe
harbor. And to make matters worse, they've spread their great
financial boat bellies over to our one little unsafe dock; now dilapidated former dock. Having the only rights to our government facilities was not enough. Now they've usurped the time
and space of the little Gustavus boaters.

Totally intimidated, the Gustavus local folks have de-
scended en masse on the Salmon River banks to build floats,
docks, paths, tie-up poles and planks on public river beaches.
Nobody blames them. For a community that depends largely on
the sea for their living, there is no place to put their boats other
than up a sand river on a high tide.

Instead of a harbor, the Feds spend millions on environmental biologists who for their salaries perform the essential task
of counting themselves while they use their private facilities at
the Park. Not to be outdone, the state spends millions on an
airport so the tourists can fly in quickly, take a retired Grey-
hound bus to the Park-leased concession hotel, stir up a cyclone
of dust en route, gawk at the funny locals wearing breather cups,

bypass the local fleet and step onto the concession cruiser via the tax-funded Park dock.

Don't get me started.

On the other hand, we're still very close to the Gustavus people and visit their mini-city often. They're the next best thing to the island. If the island sunk back into the bottom of the sea where it came from, I'd most likely join my friends again in Gustavus.

Oh, yes, I tried living in bigger places—well, more populated places, that is. This *is* big country. Everything is big—the fish, the bears, the trees, the sky, the rain, the mountains—you name it.

I was born and raised in the Rocky Mountains, a long way from seas and tides, not to mention salmon and crab. I went to college and learned to be a bureaucrat. Then I worked a few years punching time clocks at a ditch digger's wage for miserable people who commuted all year long to pay for a Buick, a mortgage and two weeks off. At the end of one very messed-up marriage with a gorgeous college sweetheart, I decided that office work in the lower forty-eight zoo in the employ of the President's palace guard wasn't exactly my thing.

One thing I did learn all those years growing up in the Rocky Mountains was how to catch fish—any kind of fish. And when I fished by myself in the middle of a creek or on the edge of a lake, I was happy. When the marriage broke up, I went fishing. Come to think of it, the marriage most likely broke up because I went fishing. Somehow I fished my way from Livingston, Montana to Southeast Alaska and picked up a job as crew on a commercial fishing boat out of Juneau.

So now I fish. I fish for fun; I fish for work. I fish because I have to fish. If I had to choose between a date with a Playboy model and a good day of fishing, I'm certain I'd opt for the latter. I fish to keep my silly skull out of a bench vice and my ass out of a sling. Before Humpback Island jumped out of the water from the bottom of Icy Strait, I fished on top of it. No doubt some of my troll gear sits on the top of that giant whale's hump up there—or lost from a bad snag on a deep drag. Ha.

Now, honest, I purposely stayed as far away from women as reasonably possible on this planet. Incredible. Who could have known that in the middle of a halibut pull, halfway up Glacier Bay, this pretty lady jumps off the Park police speed craft over to my old wood troller. Sure.

Cindy did that. And she scarcely muttered a word the whole trip. She worked her darned tail off cleaning fish and never complained. When we pulled into Excursion Inlet to sell fish, she said, "That was great." That's all she said. How could I argue?

After that, it was a good month before we touched. I mean touched without a hunk of fish slime in between.

The first night on the boat after she jumped the Park Service, she peeled off her fishy clothes not two feet away from me. I was in my sleeping bag in the other berth. She knew I watched her in the dim 12-volt light.

Then she turned around and faced me with a sort of "Oh, what the hell" look on her face, naked except for her panties. A clean T-shirt tumbled over her head and breasts. Then she sat down, tucked her feet into her sleeping bag and said, "Okay, now you've seen it. There are no mysteries, right?" She didn't let me reply and continued, "So keep your slimy hands off the goods and I'll be a fine crew for you." At that she turned off the light and went straight to sleep.

A month later, just before our kayak trip, we were selling fish at the Excursion Inlet dock. We had finished a full scrub down of the Buzz Lady after unloading its hold. Exhausted, I sat down on the port side rail with a can of pop.

Cindy saw me break, removed her rubber gloves, plopped down next to me and reached for a swallow on my can of soda. She guzzled it. I gave her my best "no shit" look. She hadn't been this forward about our personal space before.

"Thirsty," she said.

"Yeah, looks like it," I replied.

I damn near soiled my shorts when she then laid her head on my shoulder.

"And exhausted," she said.

"Guess I am, too," I answered. There were no further words.

Several seconds went by. Just when I was about to do or say something stupid, the company dock manager hollered down, "Hey, you two, better hop to it. I've got another boat due in. I need your space."

That night, anchored off Pleasant Island, before climbing in our separate berths two feet apart, we kissed—just once. Cindy climbed in her berth and rolled over like nothing strange had happened. Come to think of it, I guess I did, too.

Then we stumbled on this island by accident, in the fog, paddling a, god-forbid, kayak. Wouldn't ya know, Cindy found whales at her fingertips, wildflowers, hard living, and me. I found peace of mind, one of Mother Nature's most remarkable works of art and Cindy.

When I'm at the wheel of my boat, with a course headed west from Humpback Island past the mouth of Glacier Bay at the break of day, and the sun hits the tops of the Fairweather Mountains, there's not a better place on earth. And there's not a better woman to be found anywhere. This is heaven.

Chapter 5

Night Watching

(Tricka—Tricka)

WEEKS BEFORE THE EARTHQUAKE, AN OUT-OF-WORK pipeline biologist, weekend fisherman, and arm chair environmentalist from Juneau got messed up on his last year's flower tops, jumped aboard his twin engine cabin cruiser and set a course for Glacier Bay.

It was one of those exceptionally gorgeous Friday afternoons in late June, with not a cloud in the sky nor a whisper of breeze. He called his girlfriend, Ellen, at work to invite her along. As planned, on her way from her job at the State Office Building to the boat, she stopped at Booze Plus to grab five days' worth of bloody marys, three liters of chablis, and plenty for six nights' of martinis. When she arrived at the harbor, Brad loaded her supplies and sent her back for a rack of Rainier.

Underway, Ellen passed out in the forward cabin. Eight hours on a computer terminal deleting unemployment checks and three quick martinis while the steady drone of the boat's engines, had her dreaming of olive-colored unemployment applications. Brad rolled another one and rounded the corner of Point Gustavus to enter Glacier Bay National Park. Five minutes into the National Park his inboard engines sputtered to an unplanned stop. "Gas. I knew there was something I forgot," he complained.

Brad popped a cold Rainier to ponder his predicament. He could radio to the Park headquarters for emergency help or call for any boat in the area. The sun had dipped behind the Fairweather Range and the cool of evening was coming quickly on. For that matter, the tidal current pushed him gently in the direction of a protected shore, and he could just drop the anchor for the night and catch a passing boat for a helping hand come morning. Given his girlfriend's slumber and his own fairly comfortable buzz, the latter option felt most realistic. He didn't feel like confronting a Park ranger any time real soon, especially his old acquaintance Norm, the ranger's ranger. He cracked another beer, turned on his fathometer and waited for the tide.

Casually adrift in water several hundred feet from shore, Brad made his way out of the pilothouse towards the aft deck. As he emerged from the door a strange jolt knocked him backwards on his back to the cabin deck. His half-empty beer toppled over from the map table and drained on his forehead. A simultaneous thud below deck reminded him of Ellen, his lovely lady and sleeping ballast. "That's one way to get some life out of her," he muttered.

"Damn! what the heck was that? Brad...*Bradee?*" Ellen screamed. "Where are we?"

"Dun'no, hon. Ain't no submerged rocks around here that I know of," Brad replied. "Just take it easy. We're going to anchor up here for the night." Brad wiped his face and pulled himself up into the pilot chair. He scanned the water around the cruiser and then the fathometer screen for some clue. Nothing. Ellen emerged from below decks. "What did we hit, Brad? Are we sinking?"

Just then, toward the beach, a geyser-like spout of water whooshed upwards. A huge black and white tail lifted from the water and sunk silently away again.

Surprised, Brad grabbed his binoculars and ran for the aft deck. To his port side, whales leaped one at a time and dove to a feeding frenzy, then breached again.

"Wow!" he said. "I haven't seen whales like this in a long time."

Ellen emerged from the cabin with sunglasses in place and holding her head with her left hand. "Wow, a whole bunch of humpback whales. What's going on, honey? How come we're stopped?"

"Ran out of gas," Brad replied. He payed most of his attention to the leaping whales. "I wonder what they're feeding on?"

Ellen felt dizzy. She leaned against the rail and whined, "Brad...please." He pointed towards the beachline. A spout of water sprayed skyward.

"Ohhh! Wow!" Ellen cried out.

The current that had pushed the cruiser closer to shore had changed to propel them back the way they had come from Point Gustavus and further from the gas pump at Bartlett Cove Park headquarters. "We're losin' ground, hon. Better try to drop the anchor," Brad said. He pushed his way up to the foredeck to set loose the anchor from its moorage.

A lever released and a whoosh of chain, rope, and anchor launched from the bow of the cruiser into the water. When the coil of line hidden beneath the bow began to disappear dangerously, the boat lurched and the line tightened.

"Thank God," Brad announced.

Ellen decided to make a pot of coffee on their oil stove and found a can of corned' beef hash hidden in the cupboard. She busied herself with the domestic chores and poked her eyes and ears outdoors for an occasional view of the incredible feeding whales.

After pouring them each a hot cup of camp coffee, Ellen made her shaky way out the small cabin door to join Brad for the incredible whales. Just as she seemed to be clear of the door, a feeding whale once again lost it direction and pounded the starboard side of the boat. The coffee placed its steaming wetness directly onto Brad's stomach—both cups.

"YeeOww!" Brad exclaimed, and patted himself dry. "Between beer and coffee, I won't need a shower on this trip."

Ellen said nothing, partly in shock and fear of the whale situation and somewhat as a maneuver to avoid any more of Brad's potential the using the "poor me" over the coffee accident.

The whales had unfortunately decided to bubblenet directly above the boat's anchor. The feed must have been exceedingly thick. The boat couldn't safely move.

They were in a fix. Aside from the foaming water, Brad noticed a thick sandy mud surfacing after the thrash of the whales.

Bubblenetting is a style of whale feeding where the whales circle a school or pod of bait with great speed and ferocity. The circle creates a wall of bubbles, where the feed or bait become trapped, allowing the whales to gorge themselves luxuriously on the feed confused within the bubbles.

Whales leaped all around the small cruiser. Ellen cried. Brad held on. At one point a small whale literally leaped over the bow of the boat and then bumped the anchor line on the way back down. The boat was in tow for a second or two.

All of a sudden the splashing ceased. The humpbacks moved off, circling and diving. Chaos aboard the cruiser ended as if a storm had passed. But the whales did not move far away. They had merely taken a rest from the fury. One young whale rolled on its back near the cruiser, full and happy.

Brad and Ellen went about eating their canned hash and drinking coffee. "Are we really going to spend the night here?" Ellen asked.

"We've got to spend the night somewhere," Brad said. "This place is as good as any. Tomorrow we can get a tow to the dock for gas."

"But these whales seem to like this spot too much," Ellen complained. "It scares me."

"Oh, they won't hurt us any," Brad said. "It's this sand bottom we're anchored on that bothers me the most. Much of a wind or current comes up and we'll get moved about a little on our anchor. Could put us up on a rock on Point Gustavus. I'll stay up and keep an eye on it."

The sun had dipped behind the Fairweather range. It was now after eleven p.m. Ellen added a shot of vodka and some chocolate sauce to her coffee. Brad lit a joint and cracked open a fresh brew. They sat on the deck chairs watching the pink light of the dipping sun behind the white-capped mountains and the whales roll and dive in the near distance.

Ellen turned in after her fourth vodka chocolate brew. Brad stayed at the helm and kept an eye on his distance to shore. The anchor had drifted some but not dangerously.

At a dark twilight seen this time of year with the midnight sun rolling east beneath the horizon around the mountains of the Beartrack Inlet, another whale commotion began. First a single mature whale splashed not fifteen feet from the boat's stern. Then another smaller humpback followed. Moments later the water became a shiny murk of silver mud. And then he saw them—a small fish, maybe eight or nine inches long, flitting about in a frenzy of terror. Great mouths scooped them up in hundreds at a time.

Soon six or eight of the great whales convened to share in the feast. Water splashed everywhere under the weight of great wide tails. Shiny mud was mixed with silvery fish. Bracing himself for a jolt just in time, Brad took a wave of water onto the deck behind him. Dozens of tiny fish splashed about.

At first look, Brad figured the fish were herring. But after one landed next to his foot, he noticed it had odd fins on the side and an upturned snout, like an ocean-going, upside-down anteater. He scooped it up and placed it in the fish box behind him, then another and another. His scientific curiosity had been well whetted. What were these strange fish? And why at night? Had the whales fed on them earlier this evening, or was this a new platter of food for them? Not to mention, he didn't realize that whales fed at night, assuming they slept like other creatures.

Leaving with a deck covered in mud and small slimy fish, the flurry of whale excitement ended again, and the major number of whales moved off to starboard and safely away from the cruiser. Brad scooped what he could of the little fish into his fish box and brushed the mud out of the scupper—small holes in the deck to allow the deck to be washed down.

Anchor holding, Brad decided to call it a night at two in the morning. He crawled quietly into the v-bunk next to his snoring girlfriend. That was the one thing he couldn't excuse of Ellen— her snoring. As it went that night, the seesawing of her wheezing pipes only kept him awake a few moments. It had been a long day.

At first full light, when the sun jumped over the Beartrack Mountains to the northeast, Brad was up checking his location and anchor. The tides and the poor sand mooring had directed him toward shore. Better than being pushed out to somewhere in hell-and-gone Glacier Bay or Icy Straits. The problem facing him was that they were in ten feet of water and the tide was falling. With no power, he had no way to pull out. "Wait!" Brad exclaimed. "Kicker gas." Brad had forgotten the six-gallon tank of gas he kept for use with his small trolling "kicker" engine. He shook it. It had no more than a gallon or two.

Not wanting to disturb Ellen for the fear of potential hysterics over the situation, Brad had decided to fire up the small trolling engine, believing that the big gas guzzling engine would consume the gallon or two before he could pull the anchor.

Once fired, the small engine sputtered its way toward the anchor, pulling it easily from the sand bottom. Luckily, Brad thought, he hadn't snagged a rock or debris. No way would the kicker have pulled him loose, and he would have had to cut the anchor line, ending the trip. The anchor winch hummed the line back in, and Brad backed his way out from shore until he could put the gear in forward and set a course for the Park headquarters in Bartlett Cove. He turned the stern to the rear and headed the bow toward his destination.

Just about to breathe easy, Brad spotted a blue- and-white Park insignia labeled speed cruiser pull up from behind him. A lone young ranger in full sea-dress pulled his microphone hailer out and shouted, "Pull over, please—you, under distress in closed whale waters."

"Closed whale waters? What the criminee is a closed whale water?" Brad hollered back as he set two bumper buoys starboard.

"Sorry," the ranger said. "Is your main engine out of order?"

"No, but I'm sure as hell short on gas and could use a tow or a few gallons to get me up to the gas dock at the Park," Brad replied.

With commotion, Ellen stirred and emerged from below decks. "What's all the screaming about?" she asked.

"Just trying to get some help here from the kind young ranger, honey," Brad replied.

"Yes, but I see your anchor is muddy and wet," the ranger remarked. "Have you been anchored here for the night? This area is closed to camping by boat."

"Listen, sir, I ran out of gas," Brad said, his voice showing aggravation. I didn't have a whole lot of choice in the matter. It was dark and we were tired and hungry. The lady needed a rest and I didn't see any way out of it. You figure it out."

"Well, sir—I didn't catch your name." The ranger was busy writing down boat numbers, details.

"My name is Brad Stewart and this is Ellen Bradley. We're from Juneau, and we've made this trip a zillion times, and we never heard of closed whale waters." Brad stomped to the other side of the boat to grab a beer from the cooler. "And, by the way, what is your name?"

"Ahh, well, sir, my name is Ranger Rick Williams. I patrol the whale waters, among other things. And I'm going to give you a tow into Bartlett Cove and then cite you for violating the closed whale regulations. If you resist, I'll call for help from the other rangers and the state troopers if I have to."

At that, Ranger Rick tossed Brad a stout towline.

Brad cursed the tieing the tow line; and then being towed all the way to Bartlett Cove by this pompous jerk ranger. "Closed whale waters, my ass. Who ever heard of such a stupid damned thing. Here we are in a National Park to look at wild life from the safest piece of molecular earth there is and they tell us we can't watch the wildlife in closed waters. Shit, damn."

Ellen went below to nurse her hangover with a stout bloody mary. "Make me one, will ya', hon?" Brad asked.

By the time they arrived at the fuel dock, both Brad and Ellen had consumed three stout drinks and felt no pain or restraint. Brad tied his cruiser next to the fuel hose and jumped on the dock. Ellen watched from the deck chair.

After tying his own craft, Ranger Rick approached. "Could I see your Coast Guard papers, please, and maybe your driver's license, please?" the ranger asked.

"Now, just a minute here (burp). I didn't have any choice but to anchor there last night," Brad insisted.

"Have you been drinking? I smell alcohol," the ranger asked Brad.

"Ya,' sure, a couple of bloody mary's. "Want one?" Brad asked innocently.

"You know, it's against the law to operate a boat while under the influence," the ranger stated officially. "I'm going to have to require that you take a Breathalizer test."

"Oh, my gawd. Now what? You're going to impound my boat?" Brad shouted.

From above Brad heard familiar-sounding forthright footsteps.

"Well, Brad, where have you been? Hiding in the city, eh?" came a familiar tenor voice. "I saw you creep in here on fumes. Run out or just break a line?"

Brad turned and forced a hurried reply. "You lazy federal bum, where's your gas boy? And do something about this pesky pimple-faced ranger you dug out of some hole in a prep school. Now he wants to confiscate my damned boat for running out of gas and throw me in the clink for having a bloody mary."

"He was camped in whale waters overnight, sir. Ahh…and, and he's been drinking," Rick explained to his boss, Chief Ranger Norm Coskey.

"And out of gas," Norm added. He waved Ranger Rick off. Go check on the radios on Whale Watch Number Two, will you? I'll handle this one," Norm commanded. "Well, it seems you're the same old jerk," Norm replied. He was dressed in full uniform, as usual.

"How ya doin,' Norm? Have ya rescued any Native poachers lately?" Brad faced the ranger squarely and offered his hand for a brief but firm shake.

Norm matched the textbook version of a ranger: square head, square jaw, square haircut, and square-natured with a hidden sense of humor. Ranger Norm had been the chief of Glacier Bay Rangers for about as long as anybody could remember, maybe before it was even a national park. Blondish, green-eyed, cleanshaven with a military haircut, he wore a Roosevelt hat like he was born with it. From the Alaska look, he wore high-top brown rubber boots that he rolled down so his pant cuffs would pull over them. On his right breast pocket a gold nameplate read "N. Coskey."

"Just doing my job, Brad. Otherwise, just fine," Norm replied. "So you ran out of gas again. You need to lay off that wacky tobacky once in a while. It might be legal in this state, but it's gonna' get you stranded in a heck of a lurch some day. Remember the time we were on our way to Mckinley from

Fairbanks and you..."

"Quit preachin', sergeant. Oh, here comes the gas guy. Say, saw a nice bunch of whales down the way by Point Gustavus. I got a good look at em' when I ran out of gas and one bumped me a little. First time that ever happened," Brad rambled on.

"I knew it. You did run out of gas. Yeah, the whales have been around in good numbers this year," Norm replied. "So you saw them when you had to stop, eh? Might be something in that. I better report the whale collision."

"Something else, too." Brad climbed aboard his cruiser, opened his fish box and tossed Norm one of his strange anteater-like fish only with the nose is up-turned instead of down-turned. "The whales went nuts on 'em last night. I thought my boat would fill up with these escaping little whale bait. What are they?"

"'Tricka-tricka,' according the delicate palate of the Japanese. Here we call them Pacific Sandfish," Norm replied matter-of-factly. "They only come out of the sand at night. I hear they go for $30.00 a pound in Japan because they used up their stocks. There's a state and federal fish and game project to look at the fishery up north." Brad jumped back on dock to tend the gas boy's efforts.

"Brad, when you're done there, come over to the office to report the bump of that whale, and then I'll buy you a cup of coffee in the staff trailer," Norm said.

Gas full again, Brad paid the attendant and walked over to the Park offices. Norm was on the radio when he got there.

"Yes, captain, you can follow the west side at ten knots up to Hugh Miller. Stay 500 yards from the seal, please, over," Ranger Norm ordered into his handset.

"Man-o-man, you like this job, don't you," Brad said to Norm. "All this ordering and limiting and setting rules."

"Shut up, you old bum," Norm replied. "When did you hit

the whale?"

"I didn't hit the whale," Brad insisted. "The whale hit me—I was dead in the water. And it was about eight o'clock last night."

"Then when did the sandfish come out?" Norm asked.

"I'm not sure, really," Brad replied. "But it was late, maybe two in the morning."

Norm jotted notes on an official-looking form. "Okay, lets get that coffee. I can smell the bloody mary from here."

The staff lunch trailer was located off in the trees up the cove about a block from the office. Once inside, Brad noticed how perfectly clean the place was.

"You can't tell that anyone ever eats here," Brad said. "I wouldn't eat here either with the smell of ammonia and cleanser stinking up the food."

"Oh, just shut up, you old bum," Norm said. "With all these dirty college interns around, we have to make rules or else we'd all die of typhoid. I'm more interested in the sandfish and the whales feeding on them at night. You know we don't know a whole lot about the Pacific Sandfish in this area nor night whale feedings." He poured them both a cup of stale government coffee.

Brad took a dip and squinted. "For god's sake, you could at least have real coffee in this place." He sat the cup down. "No kidding, though. Those little fish were jumping like Mexican beans under attack. The whales were going plain nuts."

"I'll be darned," Norm replied. "Maybe a good study in this for somebody. I'll have to give it some thought, maybe call the Fish and Game guys."

"You say the Japanese pay $30.00 a pound?" Brad asked? "Zowee! That's a gold mine."

"Not in the Park whale waters," Norm replied.

"Here it would just be another scientifically interesting fauna to make some college professor a summer job."

"You can't tell me that it's okay to catch salmon, halibut, crab, and shrimp and not okay to catch sandfish," Brad replied. "You guys are just plain silly."

"I'm just speculating, "Norm said. "They're trying to close down all fishing in the Glacier Bay and I doubt the environmentalists would be real excited about a new fishery. Especially at night. From what I know, the sandfish only surface at night."

"You should've taken that Park Service job over in Juneau, Brad," Norm preached again. "We need somebody over here studying the whales. Got to keep the Greenpeace folks off our backs, you know." Norm and Brad had known each other for years. Before pipeline days, Brad worked briefly for the park service on contract up in Mckinley National Park. Norm had been there, too, at the same time, busting poachers inside the Park boundaries. Norm and Brad had the misfortune of bunking together for three months.

"Not for me—the official uniform stuff," he replied.
Brad thought he should get back to Ellen and the boat. Time to do some motoring and exploring, maybe some halibut fishing. "Well, old official junkie, I better mosey on," Brad said, and stood from his chair and poured half a cup of bad coffee down the perfectly clean sink.

"Those papers I gave you were warnings, not tickets," Norm said. "Next time Rick catches you at any of your stunts, I'll have to let him call the shots. Pick up the Park rules pamphlet down at the dock and save yourself some grief."

"Okay sergeant, thanks for the mild spanking," Brad replied. "But you better watch that young ranger you have there. He could cause World War III out of an improper turn. The kid's a little gung ho for my style. I come out here to get away from his kind."

The two men walked back through the office compound. Norm said his good-byes and Brad went for the dock. Ellen was up and brewing coffee—a good sign that her Juneau jitters had worn off a bit. She seemed to do her biggest share of drinking soon after they left Juneau on these boating jaunts.

Brad didn't pay much attention, however. He was thinking. The gas was too expensive. The thought of the whales and the strange little "tricka-tricka" stayed in his brain; the wheels were turning. He cast off the lines, gave the cruiser's bow a shove and jumped aboard.

The cruiser set a course for the east arm of the Park and Adams Inlet. Brad hadn't been there for years and Ellen had never seen it. Ellen went below to nurse a vodka coffee in hopes that it would revive her. "Where are we going, Bradee?"

Brad announced, "Someplace away from the rangers and very beautiful. You didn't miss a thing. We'll explore up through the Strawberry Islands and then try to catch the high tide into Adams Inlet. Better find some place to anchor up there for nightfall." No answer came from below. Ellen had drifted off to watch the scenery through the open-bunk berth windows. She remained silent as did Brad. Later, her body found the v-berth and Brad could hear her horrendous snoring. Two hours through the island passages, the cruiser turned east into the narrow Adams Inlet. It would be a good place to wake up in the morning, Brad thought. His mind churned from the whale and sandfish sightings. He had forgotten to roll another joint with whales and Ranger Norm's comments on his mind. Slowing to an idle to navigate the narrow passage into the face of the glacier, Brad held the wheel with a knee and began to roll a joint.

Mid-roll on a sharp corner, the aft end of a large cruiser came into view ahead. Brad dropped half the contents of his project to idle down. As he tailed closer to the boat, he heard female laughter and rock 'n' roll music.

Brad waved at two young women on the aft deck of the cruiser. The homeport markings read "San Diego, California." A beautiful young blonde waved back to him and smiled. Another young woman, a brunette, just looked at him. A bumper sticker in one of the windows said "USC."

Brad yelled to them, "I'm pulling alongside. Put out your bumpers."

"Hi there, Captain," the blonde offered in welcome.

A tanned woman who appeared to be in her mid-thirties came out of the pilothouse. "Can I help you?" she asked.

"Yeah, catch my line." Brad tossed his line at close range just as his port bow bumped the cruiser's fender.

"Got any coffee?" Brad asked in introduction. "Just looking around. I've been up here a lot, actually." He climbed aboard without asking.

"Sure," the woman said. "We're just finishing a break for dinner." Two more young women were inside the lower galley. "You up here all alone or are you hiding someone below?" she continued.

"Oh, yeah, well, someone's sleeping. What are all you beautiful young ladies doing up here?" Brad asked.

"We're studying glaciers," the blonde replied. "We have a grant from the university to watch glacial movement all summer. We're all students, except Yvonne here," pointing at the older woman. "She's our professor."

Brad was unable to speak. What a find, he thought. He took a cup of hot gourmet coffee from another of the rather stimulating crew and sat on a side bench. "Ah ha," he droned from a trance.

"Sure is a real nice day today. Water was a little rough out in the bay yesterday," Yvonne said, trying to be friendly but guarded.

"Yup," Brad said in his thinking haze. Five lovely young women on a cruiser in Glacier Bay with a grant to study glaciers. His mind churned with the possibilities. He thought of whales, of sandfish, of Norm, his sleeping girlfriend, and beautiful young college students.

"Sorry," Brad said as he came out of his deep thoughts.

"I've just had a thought. You see I'm a biologist up here on my own taking a look at this whale closure situation," he lied. "Have you seen any?"

"Not here," the blonde said eagerly. "But yesterday, down by the Park headquarters, there were three or four humpbacks feeding. We stopped the boat and watched for a long time. I love whales."

"Yes, I studied them last night, as well," Brad said nonchalantly. He couldn't keep his eyes off of the crew. The two down in the galley came up to see what the commotion was about. They were all stunning. His eyes wandered obviously.

Yvonne noticed the man's roaming gaze. "Guess we better get going, girls," Yvonne said with a little hurry. She could see his attention seemed not entirely professional. "Lots to do—lots to do, ladies. Well, it's been nice meeting you, sir." She grabbed his half-full cup and handed it to one of the galley students.

Brad was slow to respond to the hint. He got up real slow and watched the retreating lower parts of the young women. "Yeah, well, guess I better get anchored for the night," he offered. "Thanks for the coffee." He grabbed his line from the dock and jumped to his own boat. Before he landed, Yvonne had the student boat started and in gear. Only the blonde looked back and waved.

Brad's mind sailed off on a full excursion. He thought of whales, young women…young women all summer, sandfish, and maybe a real sort of job. Students were so grateful, so inquisitive, so gullible. He started the engine as the overcast daylight slipped into steady, summer twilight; no real darkness, no full daylight.

An anchor chain rattled through the Hull to break the silence. At the end of Adams Inlet, near the glacial lake, he tried to raise Ellen from her haze to tell her his idea. He knew she would be gone for the night but tried anyway.

Brad returned to the pilothouse, rolled a joint and opened

a bag of Cheetos for dinner. As dusk grew deeper the high overcast parted to the north. Brad knew it would be a special evening. He had a plan.

Reclined on the cushions next to his steering station, his presleep dreams predicted sandfish, whales, notoriety. Whale watching for fish money—what a great idea, he thought as he drifted off into the Alaska summer night.

Early morning, Ellen arose first and put on a fresh pot of coffee. Brad moaned. "Smells good, hon," he growled in his sleepy voice. "What the hell time is it?"

"Five-thirty," Ellen replied. "I slept all day yesterday, remember? You can go back to sleep if you want. I'll be quiet."

Brad did just that and Ellen put on a jacket, nabbed her coffee and went outside to see what wildlife she could see. Arctic terns flitted all around. Canadian Geese honked and squeaked on the long sand shore. Behind them a cow moose and small calf grazed on the young bunch grass. A while later a young black bear pushed his way through the willow on the far side away from the moose.

By the time Brad rolled out of his berth, the larger animals had disappeared. "You missed a real wildlife show, Brad," Ellen remarked when she heard him stir. She moved in for a warm-up on the coffee and met Brad at the little diesel stove. "I want to go halibut fishing today—okay?" she blurted out.

"We can do that," Brad replied. "I know a good hole just outside the inlet."

On the early incoming high tide, Brad and Ellen safely motored the cruiser out of Adams Inlet, then anchored near a small island. A large commercial sport fishing charter boat was anchored close by so Brad figured he had the right spot. Their poles were rigged, and Brad had brought along some bait herring. He used the herring on Ellen's hook, but on second thought put a sandfish on his. "We'll see if halibut like the taste of these little upside down anteaters as much as the whales," he said.

Not long after their line and hooks had bounced bottom, a clatter rang out from the sport charter. A Japanese fellow had a hold of a whopper halibut, at least a 200-pounder. Hooks and gaffs were flying; the boat was a buzz of activity. Brad heard the charter crew call the successful fisherman "Captain San Diego." He thought that to be an odd name for a Japanese fellow and a coincidence since the all-women boat from the night before home ported by the same name. That got him thinking again about all his schemes.

Brad's full mind became distracted when his pole gave a major jerk. The line ran out of the reel with breakneck speed. "Aha, the sandfish," he exclaimed.

Ellen reeled her line back to allow elbow room for what looked like a big one on Brad's pole. As soon as it was near the top he handed ellen the pole and went for his shark hook gaff. The gaff struck the fish heartily and soon a hundred pounds of fish flopped on the deck. Ellen shouted for joy. Brad boasted his sandfish. Ellen put her line back in the water and soon hauled in a forty-pounder.

The Japanese fellow yelled over in full, unaccented English, "Nice fish there, guys, but I'll bet tonight's dinner at the Park Lodge that mine doubles your weight."

Brad hollered back, "Your fish is bigger, yes, but not twice as big. No way. You're on." Both boats pulled up anchors. "See you at the dock at five."

A trip across to the west side of Glacier Bay for a try at a king salmon failed. Brad and Ellen gave up about three in the afternoon and made their way to the lodge for a free dinner. As they pulled in alongside the dock so did the big charter with Captain San Diego.

After tie-down, the big fish were hauled overboard to the cleaning tables and the scale. Brad's fish came in at 108 pounds before gutting and cleaning. The boastful Captain San Diego's fish fell short of the 200 pound mark by one pound. Brad and

Ellen had won the bet. "Well, dinner's certainly on me," the captain admitted. "I'll meet you at the restaurant at six-thirty."

At dinner the topic turned to the fishing technique and the particular bait used. "I used my secret jig," Captain S. boasted.

"Well Ellen here, caught hers on our secret herring rig," Brad replied. "But then, I got mine on whale bait."

"Whale bait? What in the world is whale bait?" the captain asked. "I thought they consumed everything that floated around these parts."

Brad went into his story from last night and described the little fish with the turned up nose.

"You mean tricka-tricka?" the captain shouted. "You got a gold mine there, boy. Where did you find them?"

Brad wouldn't say. "Secret," he replied. But he went into his story of running out of gas "somewhere" in the bay at night and about the whales that came up after the odd little fish with a fury.

The captain twisted in his seat and ordered another round of after dinner drinks. He fidgeted nervously as if he was being denied the most important part of the story. "I tell you, this is a gold mine," the captain repeated.

Dinner ended with the captain giving Brad his card and Brad scribbling his address on a lodge cloth napkin. The captain begged Brad, "You keep me posted on the tricka-tricka," and returned to his room at the lodge.

Brad and Ellen headed for the cruiser.

Nine months later, Brad had received a grant from Fish and Game, a stipend from a Japanese fishing interest, and a grant from the Park Service to study bott the sandfish and the whales' night behavior. Good ol' Ranger Norm had helped him get the inside track, and Captain San Diego connected him with one of his Japanese friends. He had also managed to talked the university in Juneau into offering credits to students for the study, and Brad successfully solicited the commitment of the university to send five biology students on a summer-long research project.

The successful applicants for the class would receive four credits and a stipend from the grant. It was up to Brad to select from the finalists those he felt could address the rigorous nature of the environment and the closeness of the research boat. From a list of twenty submitted by the fish biology faculty, Brad picked five. They were all female. One of them was a striking blonde who had run into Brad the summer before in Adams Inlet. She was now a senior fish biologist at the University of Alaska Southeast in Juneau. Her name was Cindy and she loved Glacier Bay. Juneau was closer to the bay than San Diego.

Since the students were all female, Brad promised the University that there would be a woman aboard to chaperon. Brad encouraged Ellen from the start.

The first day on the research vessel—Brad's old cruiser with fresh paint—Ellen introduced herself, poured a bloody mary, and went permanently below. In fact, most onlookers and Park Service personnel never knew she was aboard the entire summer. Brad waited till Ellen was routinely stuporous and began the first lesson of survival in the northern wilderness.

To his lovely crew eager for their first lesson, memo pads in hand, Brad announced: "We must all learn to survive in cold water." At that he took off every stitch of his clothing and jumped overboard. "Come on in," he beckoned, "the water is colder than hell."

"Oh, for heaven's sake," Cindy said. She turned and went into the pilothouse.

The others, however, believing this to be a journey into the last frontier, chucked their clothes and jumped in. Brad, although freezing to near death, was in ecstasy. This was his calling, his mission. He climbed out and watched in awe as the young ladies frolicked in the icy water. Before getting dressed he called to Cindy to bring them towels.

Cindy fetched the towels from below. On her return to

the aft deck she asked Brad, "Is this research?"

"No. But it's part of the experience," Brad replied with self-assurance. "It's required for research from this boat. A person needs to know how to survive in this country."

"I'll send for my swimming suit, thank you," she replied. "Survival in this country may necessitate hand-to-hand combat. In the meantime, you could use a cold shower?" Cindy turned and went below.

A month into the summer project, not a day had passed that Brad hadn't required a naked swim in the glacial waters. He usually stayed on deck saying that someone had to keep a look-out.

Cindy refused to comply with the swim requirements. And Ellen didn't have the foggiest notion what was going on above deck until one day Cindy went below and dragged her, half-asleep and hungover, to topside. Brad was basking in the radiance of his required event and Ellen fainted dead away at the sight.

One day at anchor in Bartlett Cove, Cindy protested the nature of Brad's bizarre research to Ranger Norm. The ranger only raised his eyebrows and shook his head. When Cindy insisted that someone look into the problem, Norm referred her to the Park superintendent.

Cindy left the superintendent's office with an apology from the top guy and an offer to finish her credited course with a paid summer position as an assistant to the chief biologist.

Brad's research, nonetheless, continued with no clear scientific findings. Between swims, the students got to see, count, and name a bunch of whales. Pacific Sandfish occasionally arose from the depths of their hiding places to be eaten en mass by the night-feeding humpback and orca. Most of the night feedings were sighted outside of the Park boundaries in the sandy- bottomed Icy Straits. The summer research did prove three things: Whales feed at night. Whales feed on a good number of the previously unknown Japanese delicacy, "tricka-tricka," or Pacific Sandfish and that beautiful female students can swim naked in the cold waters of Glacier Bay.

The net result of the research became incredibly famous. While nothing really pointed to the need, the Park Service closed the bay to all motorized boat traffic at night in speculation that the boats may have an impact on the whales' feeding. In federal regulation, it reads something like this: "The critical research of Mr. Brad Stewart has indicated a need to err, if at all, on the night safety of the humpback whale and the rare Pacific Sandfish."

Those familiar with the problems of National Parks down south are aware of the crowding of tourists, campers, Winnebago's, and people teasing bears. Wilderness criminals steal bear gallbladders elk antlers. In Glacier Bay, the Park Service had only a pesky glut of researchers and biologists.

According to Cindy, the night boat regulations imposed by the Park Service are a masked attempt on the part of Park personnel to prevent normal people from enjoying the National Park.

Ranger Rick was elated with his new night cruiser. He could pick up a drifting rowboat on his new sonar and the engine horsepower more than doubled.

According to Norm, whale harassment didn't start with weekend tourists. It started with Brad. "There got to be so many damned research boats and biologist types out there studying and poking that the poor whales spooked out as far away as they could from Glacier Bay," Norm said.

Brad went on to develop a minor Pacific Sandfish fishery outside the Park boundary.

"Lucky for most of us, though," Cindy proclaimed, "we restrict researchers, Park Service employee's and related club members from harassing the wildlife around Humpback Island. If you want to see plenty of whales, forget the government and corporate mega-cruise-ship- infested waters of restricted Glacier Bay and cruise just outside the Park boundary around Point Adolphus or Humpback Island. The whales love to show off to regular whale watchers or otherwise normal human beings, their small boat engines, and ever-clicking cameras. And if you're lucky and boating at night, you'll see an occasional tricka-tricka being chased by a very large predator."

Chapter 6

Nobody Ever Said

"YOU'RE HAVING A STUPID COW," HE ANNOUNCED with his usual calm.

"I am not, Tad. God, you're an idiot!" Beth screamed. She stomped her right foot on the wood kitchen floor.

"Bullshit. Cow doodo dribbles from your mouth. Take a big deep breath and think what you're saying," Tad replied. "And yes I might be an idiot." He backed away from the wood spool table with his cup in hand. The coffee steamed on the kitchen wood cookstove. A rolled cigarette smoldered in a sardine tin ashtray.

"I wish you wouldn't smoke that awful garbage. It makes me sick." Beth stared blankly at the curling blue smoke. She shook from head to toe.

"Your endless cow pies make me sick, Beth. Get a life." Tad lifted the pot to his cup, then set it off to the cool side of the stove.

A fresh strawberry pie sat cooling on the window ledge above the sink. Beth felt like a volcano. He was always so damned calm. She wished he would hold her and ask her how he could change. But no, all he could do was tell her to get a life. What life? Tad was always gone. She had an urge to throw the pie straight into his pompous face. "You bet I have a pie. I baked it just for you. For the big fisherman I never see. Here's a pie for you." It burned her hand when she grabbed it without a hot pad. Beth lofted it squarely at her husband's chest. A short laugh flew from deep within her belly. A pained sigh followed.

Boiling coffee and steaming red goo trickled down Tad's entire front. The smell of hot strawberries and canned coffee filled the room. He was too mad to scream in pain, too shocked to move or utter a single exclamation.

Beth faced her husband. A tear trailed from her eye down her cheek. They glared at each other for what seemed like the cycle of an Alaskan moon.

"Thanks for the pie and coffee, dear," Tad drawled to break the silence. A slight quiver of pain shuddered from the center of his torso. "Guess I'll go fishing. Too messy around here, cow shit, strawberries and all."

Beth started to come out of her trance. "Wa...what do you think this is all about?" she cried.

Tad cut her off. "Don't start up again, Beth." He tracked reddish pie ruins and brown coffee puddles to the towel rack next to Beth. He avoided her eyes and wiped hastily.

"Fishing! I think you're sick. You fish every day. For fun you fish. For work you fish. If there's time, you fish. Why don't you go marry a fish? I'm leaving. If you get time, catch a fish and shove it up...ah, well, eat it for dinner. I hope you get salmonella."

Tad slammed the door behind him. Tears swelled his eyelids but he refused to let the dam break. Instead he ran to his boat.

Beth stood by the sink. She couldn't move. Her tears flowed freely now as did a spasmodic noise from her throat.

Moments went by. Beth had no idea how long, but the broken pie and coffee goo was cold when she finally knelt down to wipe it up with the towel Tad had thrown at her. The crying sound revived when she dropped some of the fresh strawberry on her jeans. Whimpers turned to chuckles and then finally to "Yes...yes."

Tad let out frustrated curses as he motored his way half around the island. He set his trolling lines on the western side;

no matter there wasn't a sign of a good bait fish school, or bleeps on his fish finder. By the time he reached the southern shore he felt real bad—like real, real bad. Maybe she was right. He had probably been ignoring Beth since the season began— hell, since the honeymoon was over. Maybe longer. Even when he sat out on a closure, problems with the boat hydraulics and trouble with getting his money from the fish buyer had consumed his energy. Beth finally blew her stack when he announced he had to make a run to Sitka for parts. He didn't think to invite her along. "Stupid, stupid," he grunted.

Tad tried to reach her on the radio. He heard no answer from the home set. Later on, he tried again with no luck. Fisherman Frank overheard his call and broke in to say, "Cindy said she saw Beth hop a flight for Juneau this afternoon. Anything I can do? Over." "No, Frank. Guess not. Just kick my butt the next time you see me. Better yet, just shoot me," Tad answered. "Juneau, huh? Over." Tad remembered seeing the plane come and leave the island when he was putting out his lines.

Frank didn't have a clue how to continue the conversation. "Yup, Juneau, by golly," Frank replied. "How's your drag there? Over."

"Not much here, Frank. I'm just keeping the lines used to feeling wet. Might go in for the day. Over."

"Yup, same thing over here," Frank acknowledged. "I've been out six days. Might just sell the few skinny ones that took pity on me and see if my wife still remembers my name. Over."

Tad winced in pain. Enough talk over the radio. By now the whole Icy Strait fleet knew he had marriage problems. "Yeah, I'll talk to you later, Frank. Thanks for the scoop. I'm clear and back to channel sixteen."

Frank clicked the microphone twice to signal he would get off the line and do the same. He figured to know soon enough what Beth's flight to Juneau was all about.

Tad returned home not knowing what to expect inside. He

was surprised to find no sign of splattered coffee and strawberry pie. Instead he found the kitchen neat as a pin. He searched the usual places and found no note. He moved on to the bedroom upstairs. Her wardrobe and personals were in complete order. Again, no note. Confused and exhausted Tad sprawled on the bed in his fishing clothes. Sleep came swiftly.

Beth couldn't believe she was doing this. She had saved the money from most of her art sales carefully for a trip outside this winter. She wanted to visit her parents in Wisconsin and maybe look for a place in the sun for a week or two. She hadn't been home since her marriage two years ago. Her parents and little sister came all the way to Alaska for the wedding.

Tad said he might go along with her if it was after the deer hunt and before spring king season. But now she was about to give most of her savings to a religious communal farmer in Hoonah.

After her plane landed in Hoonah with a bump on the gravel runway, Beth made her way directly into the air charter office in hopes of using the telephone there. A beautiful young Native woman smiled at her and asked, "Can I help you?"

"Yes, please," Beth replied. "Could I use your phone?"

"Sure. Want some coffee?" The air clerk pointed to a fancy pot on a table. "My name is Mary Williams. I work here. Ha." The young woman laughed as though the concept of work was funny. "I got the coffee from Juneau. You know, the gourmet place. It's really good. It's my pot too. Ha, ha."

Beth moved toward the telephone Mary placed on the small counter between them. "I need to make this call first," Beth answered politely.

"Who do you want to call? Uh...maybe I can help," the clerk interjected. "I know everybody in Hoonah, you know." She giggled again, somewhat embarrassed.

"A man named Clay. He lives on the hippie farm, and I have his number, thank you." Beth grabbed for the phone and quickly dialed. Mary pretended to work on flight schedules, ears alert.

"Hi, this is Beth Neff from Humpback Island. I talked to a man named Clay. Is he there?"

Beth turned away from the counter for an attempt at privacy. Her foot wiggled a fast-paced rhythm while a woman went to track down the leader of the commune. The woman's voice had been polite, very sweet.

"Yes, this is Beth Neff. I called you about buying the cow yesterday, and I brought a check with me. Can I see her?"

"Ha," the clerk started to giggle. Then she held her mouth in a failed attempt to hide her laughter.

Beth turned to glare at Mary. She put her hand over the mouthpiece. "Please," she whispered to Mary and turned around. To the receiver she said, "I'll wait outside."

Beth turned to place the phone back on the receiver. Mary was still trying to suppress her funny bone.

"Excuse me. So what's so damned funny?" Beth asked in an irate tone.

"You're buying one of those ugly old cows?" Mary asked between blurts.

"Yes, I am."

"What do you want a cow for."

"None of your business, really," Beth replied and then had second thoughts. "Actually, it's for my husband—sort of a present."

Mary raised her eyebrows and started to say something more. A loud popping noise distracted them. Mary jumped from her chair. "It's Buck," she screamed over the noise. "Wonder what he's doing all the way over here?"

Beth was happy for the distraction. She waited a moment to get some separation and then followed the clerk out the door.

A shiny helicopter touched down near the office. The blades from the helicopter wound slowly to a stop. A lean, dark, and very handsome man stepped down from the pilot's door.

Mary jumped in front of Beth as they neared the strapping pilot. She grabbed his arm and spoke close to his ear. "Buck, what are you doing here?"

"Who's this pretty woman?" he drooled, pointing at Beth over by the little office.

"Oh," Mary answered, shocked into politeness. They walked up closer to the office porch where Beth pretended lack of interest. "Buck, this is Beth from Humpback Island. She's here to see a man about a cow. Ha, Ha, Ha."

Beth squinched her face up in embarrassment. "Well, really, I just...," she tried to say.

"A cow, huh?" Buck questioned, pushing his hand out to Beth's. "Real nice to meet ya, Beth." He sort of half winked as he gently shook her hand.

Buck's manner made her feel more at ease. "Yes, nice to meet you, too," Beth replied. She was blushing, and it was noticeable in spite of efforts to prevent it. "The cow's a present for my husband," Beth added. She turned to walk back to the air charter office, hoping that the crimson in her face would fade with not looking at him. Buck and Mary took the cue to follow.

Mary put her arm again in Buck's. She leaned her head on his shoulder as they walked. "You didn't tell me why you're here in Hoonah, Buck."

"The boys up on the cliff want some film, and I needed to see something other than smelly surveyors climbing mountains. Of course, as always, you have more than fulfilled my wildest dreams for a diversion." Buck was straight-faced.

"Oh, shut up, you stupid flirt." Now Mary blushed. She pulled her head and arm away for effect and hurried in front. "I have some fancy coffee on," Mary shouted back without turning.

Just as Beth turned the knob of the office door, a large stake-bed pickup truck turned up onto the gravel airport skirt towards her. Again, she was relieved to have a diversion from Mary and her friend. She could see the animal's head peering over the cab. The truck pulled to a stop immediately beside her. The driver's door opened to reveal a short and muscular man with a full head of curly brown hair tied in a ponytail. Beth approached him from around the hood.

"Hi, there," the man said in a robust voice. "You must be Beth Neff from Humpback. I'm Clay, and this lovely critter in back is Ida Mae." Clay pointed to the rear of the truck. The cow snorted over the cab. Clay motioned for Beth to follow him around closer to the side of the truck. "Isn't she a beauty?" He put his hand through the truck's slats and ran his fingers up the cow's sagging belly.

"Ah, well...yes, I guess," Beth replied. "Does she have a name? Oh, excuse me—Ida Mae, right?"

"Yes, ma'am," Clay exclaimed. The cow immediately turned towards them. Her teats swooshed with her movement. "Her mom came from Idaho and she was born in May two years ago," Clay continued. "She's gonna be a good milker, Beth. Would you like to pet the lady?"

"Ah, nah, that's okay. She looks fine," Beth replied apologetically. "I have the check right here." Beth handed Clay the envelope from her pocket. "When can you bring her to the island?"

"Next week if the weather's not too nasty. Maybe—oh say...Tuesday?" Clay answered. "Our little tow barge can't take a wave more than a four footer."

"Could you keep it sort of quiet?" Beth added. "This is a surprise for my husband. He's a fisherman. You know, he stops at the cold storage here in Hoonah." "Sure will," a male voice boomed from behind her. It was Buck. "Yep, sure is a nice cow you have here, Beth," Buck chided. "It must have cost a pretty penny to buy a heifer like this baby."

"No, not really," Beth replied.

"That's right," Clay added. "But she's not a heifer, at least not for long. She's got a calf in her. Two for the price of one and soon all the milk you and the neighbors can use."

Beth turned quickly to face Clay. "You didn't tell me that on the phone," Beth said.

"You told me you wanted one that could milk. No calf, no milk," Clay answered.

"Oh," Beth exclaimed.

Buck laughed. "I'm leaving," he announced. "If you're done here, Beth, I'll give you a lift back to your island."

"I have a reservation on the five o'clock. But thank you," Beth replied.

Mary piped in from behind them. She stood at the office door. "I could cancel your five o'clock. Juneau just called and said you're the only one. The pilot could knock off for the day if you changed your plans. On the other hand, I hate to see Buck take off so soon."

Beth reluctantly looked to Clay for a sign of permission.

"We'll see you on Tuesday, Mary," Clay announced. "If the weather's bad, look for us on the next nice day." He climbed back into his truck and was gone.

Beth felt a little queasy. She deemed it her last-ditch effort to get Tad's attention. Pretty crazy to buy a cow. It would be the very first cow on Humpback Island, and just to make a stupid point. Consider it a joke to keep my husband amused. She watched the cow truck turn up the road into the tall spruce trees.

Buck and Mary had already gone into a playful show of affection. Beth turned to see them playing tag with each other's knees. She couldn't tell if they really meant it or went through this romantic game to pass the time.

"When are we leaving?" Beth asked the pair.

"I've got to visit the store for the film first," Buck replied. "Do you want to come along for the ride or stay here with Mary? I won't be long. Hey, Mary, can I use your Bronco?"

Mary replied first. "Stay on the road and away from the bar."

"Come on," Buck said to Beth, soliciting her with his finger over his shoulder.

Beth decided to kill the time out of the reach of Mary's non-stop giggling. Buck, heaven forbid, was the lesser of the two miseries. She reluctantly made her way to the Bronco.

Buck waited at the wheel. "It's sure nice to meet you, Beth," he said. "Can I take you somewhere besides the store?"

"No, the store's fine. I'm just along for the scenery," Beth answered.

"No, you brought the scenery," Buck added. He did not look at her.

Beth blushed.

The beginnings of the city of Hoonah passed by. School kids were playing in the street. Beth had never been here during the school year. She had stopped at the airport en route to Juneau once or twice, but had never left the small plane. She came to the Hoonah harbor during the summer three times with her husband to ice the boat or pick up parts. Now, for some reason, the little community seemed different in the fall. Maybe it was all the kids, swinging school bags on the way home.

Buck pulled the Bronco up to the side of the store. Children ran in and out of the door with their afternoon snacks. Teenagers jostled for advantage and position against the wall. "Want anything?" he asked Beth as he opened the driver side door.

"No not really. Well, maybe a How to Have a Cow book." Beth got out of the Bronco and followed Buck in.

Separating at the door, Buck went for the film and Beth went for a soda. They met again at the soda cooler.

"Did you find a cow book?" Buck asked. He wondered if he could ever loosen this woman up. He couldn't remember her pushing a real smile.

"I was kidding," Beth answered.

"Are you sure you really want that cow?" Buck asked. "You

don't seem very excited about it. "Does your husband want a cow?"

"He thinks I already have one: almost every day I have one." Beth paid for her pop and walked out the door of the store. She heard Buck break out into a chuckle as the door closed behind her.

In the Bronco Buck said nothing. At least she had a sense of humor. But still no smile. He'd seen her blush. He wondered what in the hell would push her buttons.

Buck pulled up to the little airport office and turned off the key. "That cow will be one hell of a big chunk of fisherman's bait," he replied.

"He won't use it for bait," Beth protested.

Buck climbed from the vehicle. "I'll meet you by the chopper," he declared. He decided to take his lumps for now and retreat till he had her in the chopper.

Beth sat in the car immobilized by the conversation. To her the cow was a retaliatory joke; a very big one. Now she wondered if it would backfire on her.

When Buck came out the door of the office, Beth jolted from her daze to follow him. Buck didn't rib her anymore, nor did he ask her why she still sat in the car. When they approached the helicopter, Buck held the door for her to climb in. She sat in the co-pilot seat next to him. He handed her headphones and showed her how to use the mouthpiece to talk. Buck obviously thought he was a skilled professional—maybe he really was, she thought. Beth watched as he checked the instruments and fired the engine. Until now, she saw him only as a pesky womanizer.

The chopper lifted off gently. Mary waved them off from below with her big grin. The ground sank beneath as the clearcut forests loomed in front of them. Buck lifted the chopper over a bald hill and back down to skim across the water of Icy Straits. A group of humpback whales surfaced directly ahead in unison. Buck spotted them and sank slowly to hover not more than fifty feet from the creatures. Beth nearly jumped out of her seatbelt when one of the whales breached clear out of the water.

"My God, Buck!" she exhaled.

Buck took the cue and moved the stick forward. Approaching Point Adolphus, Buck pointed to another group of whales. Fishing boats trolled just off the pod of whales.

Beth spotted her husband's troller off Lemeisure Island. Her mood turned suddenly darker.

"Is that your husband there?" Buck asked.

Beth nodded nervously.

"Lets check him out," Buck suggested, and before Beth could protest, the chopper was on the boat like bees on clover.

Tad came from the wheelhouse to see what the commotion was all about. His lines worked behind his slow troll. Coho salmon jumped all around. He was on a bite with a good catch already aboard. Tad waved, not yet seeing the passenger.

Beth waved back, not knowing what else to do.

When Tad recognized her, he pointed his finger to his wife's face, then hit his forehead with an open hand. He waved again and then held both arms up to signal his confusion.

Buck took the cue to swerve off. Without a word the chopper made a straight heading for the island. Beth waited for the blades to grind to a complete stop. Buck removed his headgear and opened the door.

"Better come flying again, Beth," Buck announced. "I knew you'd like it."

"Maybe," Beth answered. "Thank you." She smiled and made her way from the helicopter, for a time half slouched to avoid the motionless blades, down the path towards her small house. She heard the engine fire and the blades begin to cut the air.

Beth felt relieved to come home after two days away. Her first night in Juneau was awful. The motel by the airport was noisy. She couldn't sleep till after three in the morning. After the call to the farm in Hoonah that evening, she spent most of the night crying through sitcoms on the first television she had seen since last spring's on the trip to Sitka. Then she pondered the professional flirtations of the pilot, Buck and the goofy conversations with the airline receptionist, Mary, in Hoonah.

Now, home on the island, best of all, Tad was not here yet. While he knew she was back, he'd have to sell his fish before returning. That gave her a few hours to plot her eventual uncomfortable greeting. She wondered what Tad would do or say.

Beth filled a hot tub and plopped into the steamy water as if her body had been chopping wood all day for the winter heat supply. Soaking, her mind wandered from Tad to Buck. Tad was raw, uncalculating, mild tempered and as regular as the bloom and death of a dandelion blossom. Buck was cool, flashy, and cunning. Each of Buck's smiles, winks, and questions would inevitably bring him to some wicked conclusion. Tad didn't have a manipulation or a hidden agenda for a thing. Sometimes Beth felt a little bored with Tad's complete openness—there were no surprises.

Beth's daydreaming took her back to gazing on an open deck of fish from a shiny helicopter. A riff-raff barge in tow loomed into the picture. A cow stood on the deck. Buck laughed. "What in God's name will you do with a cow?" she shouted. Her own voice brought her to earth. The water had turned cool.

Tad walked in just after dark. Beth sat on the little maroon overstuffed couch she made him haul on his boat from Juneau. Dressed in an Indian pattern blanket she sipped herbal tea. Tad smelled of fish.

"Hi stranger," Tad said. "I had a good catch today."

"I saw that," Beth acknowledged.

Tad took off his brown rubber boots and pulled the rag wool sweater over his head. He faced her directly. "Where did you find a chopper?"

"Free ride from Hoonah. It wasn't planned," Beth added. She sipped her tea and drew in her breath.

"Hoonah?" Tad questioned. "I heard you went to Juneau."

"I did. Then I stopped in Hoonah on the way home. Ahh...by the way, it's nice to see you, Tad."

"I was worried," Tad said. He turned away to remove more smelly clothing. "I tried to call you on the radio, but Frank said you had gone. Pretty weird." He made his way to the bathroom unbuttoning his fishy jeans. "I better wash the slime off. Don't move." He felt conspicuous, nervous, and almost wished he'd spent the night on the boat.

Beth got up to freshen her tea, then left it on the counter. She pushed the door open into the bathroom. Tad's fishy underwear and jeans lay on the bathroom floor. She picked them up, emptied his pockets, and put his clothes in a wash hamper outside the bathroom door.

Tad watched Beth move from his steamy tub. The Indian blanket had fallen over one shoulder to reveal her nakedness. She was truly beautiful. He noticed no sign of the argument from two days ago. Why did she stay here on this little island in the middle of nowhere? She could have much more. He felt as though he was not good enough.

The blanket slipped to the floor to cover only her waist down. Beth knelt by the tub and leaned forward to caress his face.

"I'm sorry, Beth," Tad whispered. "I missed you."

Beth ignored the part of her that was hurt and confused. She pushed herself closer and wondered if by doing so she would get more confused.

"I'm sorry, too," she said. A wry smile came over her face.

"What's so funny?" Tad asked.

"Just us," Beth answered. "I have a surprise for you." At that she let the blanket fall from her waist to the floor.

Chapter 7

The Winter Dance

WHEN THE HOONAH HIPPIE FARM MINI BARGE TIED up to Humpback Island's tiny dock, former ranger Norm Coskey was the only one on hand to meet it. His oversized aluminum skiff, full of most of his worldly belongings was tied to the other side. Piece by piece, book by book, chart by chart, Norm moved it all via a small plywood cart the quarter mile to his newly erected, undone retirement cabin home.

After exactly 30 years of federal service, Norm had given his last bureaucratic year to the Park. No more did he arrest tourists for littering, defoliating, and harassing. At the age of fifty-two he had seen enough government bullshit, from Yosemite to Denali, to fill a Princess Cruise ship or two. At a potluck/work party to finish his roof he pronounced, "God save me from the Department of the Interior, for I have given my life to memos, tickets, and forms."

Norm took a break from his retirement move to Humpback Island to help Clay tie up the barge and the antique cruiser that pulled it. "What are you needing here?" Norm asked in a held over, habitual officious tone.

"Delivering a cow to Beth Neff and this person to whatever," Clay answered. "Have you seen the Neffs?"

Just then a tall, rather mangy man with thinning long dark hair and a scruffy beard stepped from the barge to the dock. He was dressed in camouflage combat gear and brown rubber boots with a dirty red bandanna tied around his head. He half-nodded to Norm, then unloaded three green duffel bags, a large frame pack, five full gun cases, a tent, a large plastic container, a grocery box, and a camp stove.

"Oh, yeah," Clay added, "this is John somebody. He decided he didn't like too Hoonah much."

Norm checked out John with a cocked eyebrow. "Huh... yes," he said.

"What about Ms. Neff?" Clay asked again.

Norm continued his scrutiny of John. The scruffy man self-ignored the retired ranger and began to relay his belongings up the dock to the beach. Norm switched his attention to the cow and Clay. "I think the Neffs are dragging in beach logs for firewood. They could be on the other side of the island. Most likely they'll be back around soon before dark sets in," he replied.

Clay jumped to the barge. He loosened the tethers on the cow and said, "Well, maybe you or John-somebody up there could help me get this critter up to the Neffs' house. Do you know where their house is?"

"Sure do, sir," Norm replied. "It's just up the beach a ways. You better believe that this cow will cause a little excitement."

"She's a good cow," Clay proclaimed. "I brought her along some feed, too. It's in plastic bags, so I'll just leave it here above the dock on the beach." He handed Norm the tether. "Here, hang onto her while I set out some planks."

John had finished moving his gear up on the beach and sat on his plastic container assessing the October landscape. Dark clouds moved with serious quickness across the sky to the south. A roll to the sea meant wind from somewhere in the distance.

The sweet cloud of marijuana smoke caught a downdraft. Weird John inhaled deeply, and looked out over the water to the sand shore of Gustavus. There was little sign of human occupation past the two men on the small dock. "This is it," he said between puffs. "This is really it."

Clay heard John's mumbling and smelled the sweet aroma of his cigarette. "Hey, John," Clay yelled. "Could you help us with this cow?"

John got up slowly from his plastic chair and ambled down the hill. He was tall and his long hair fell below his camouflage collar. He offered Norm a hit from his rolled cigarette while he petted the side of the cow through the slats of the barge.

"No thanks," Norm said with a nervous smile and quick negative shake of his head.

Clay saw the offer. "I'll take a hit," he said and put out his thumb and index finger. He took a long toke and held it in till he choked. "Oh, yeah, good stuff." He returned the stub of a joint. John took one last hit and stuffed the remainder in his shirt pocket.

Clay and John maneuvered two large wood planks into place between the dock and the barge. When Clay felt the boards were secure, he took the tether from Norm. "Okay, lead the way, Norm," Clay proposed. "See ya later, John. Good luck."

John gave the cow another slow rub on her swollen side. "Nice cow," he blurted, then ambled up the dock toward his gear. He pulled the stub of a joint from his pocket and lit up.

Clay and Norm led the cow up the beach toward Tad and Beth's house. Norm asked Clay, "So tell me a couple of things. First, what in the hell is this cow all about?"

"You've got me," Clay replied. "Some sort of present for Tad or something. Beth flew over a few weeks ago wanting to buy a cow. I think it's a sort of secret gift or something."

"Okay...well...then what's this John-somebody doing here?" Norm continued. "He seems a little iffy, if you know what I mean. There's a kind of strange look in his eyes."

The cow stopped on a gradual incline. Clay gave her a nasty yank and she reluctantly inched forward.

"Weird John? That's what the Hoonah folks called him.

He came on the ferry from Juneau a few weeks ago. Stayed by himself up in the trees by Whitestone until the loggers asked him to move on. People say he's a decorated Vietnam vet that doesn't like crowds. On the way here from Hoonah the guy didn't say more than ten words. All he did was grumble to himself and smoke that awesome dope. Didn't seem dangerous though and he did take a serious liking to the cow."

The two men and the cow came to a small cabin nestled in a tangle of new willow and alder. Boat gear hung from the walls and a diesel generator thumped from a small shed to the left rear. To the right side of the cabin stood a smoke house and a clothes drying contraption constructed of sturdy beach poles and old halibut longline rope. Clay tied the cow up to one of the beach poles and asked, "Could you tell Beth the cow has some feed down at the dock? She better be sure to get some more before winter. Tell her to call if she needs any advice. Really sorry to bother you about this Norm, but I better get back before it blows much more. That little barge can't take much water, and I see a storm coming in from the south."

"No problem there, Clay," Norm replied. "A unique duty for me; I guess it's a little different for everybody here. There aren't many cows around, just a couple across the water by the Gustavus Inn."

"She'll be no problem. Just feed her and put a tarp up over her in the rain. See ya." Clay hurried back to the dock.

Norm decided to hang around awhile and make sure the cow didn't pull the yard apart. He chose a damp firewood round for a chair and placed his gloves flat on the cut edge so the moisture would not wet his jeans. The cow just stood there, occasionally putting her head down to chew on the lush grass still green from the summer. He saw Weird John coming up the trail past the Neffs' cabin. John half nodded again as he hiked past him. Norm winced and wondered where the guy would put up his tent, hopefully not too close to his own place.

Norm filled an old bucket with water from the Neffs' rain barrel and set it next to the cow. He ran his hand along the critter's bulging side. He knew enough to suspect the cow to be pregnant. He thought he'd like to be on hand for the Neffs' arrival.

The big critter didn't seem too interested in bolting away, let alone venture beyond the next clump of grass. Norm gave the cow a brief pat on the nose, then made his way back to the dock. He remembered his own task. The little bicycle-wheeled cart used to move his supplies was full already, awaiting the next haul to his undone cabin. His skiff remained secure.

Just as he got to the top of the dock ramp with his load, Tad and Beth's boat rounded the corner with a dozen or so large drift logs in tow. Norm glanced down at the cow feed piled by his feet. A blue plastic tarp lay on top of his cart. He remembered the "secret surprise" Clay had mentioned and quickly spread the "N Coskey" stenciled tarp over the bags of feed. He waved to the Neffs and continued on his way up the beach. Maybe he'd pass by the cow scene on the last cartload before dark.

Beth hopped over the rail to the dock to tie down the fishing boat. The logs drifted skillfully alongside the starboard side, opposite the dock. Once secured, Tad jumped from his boat and ran up to the beach. The Neffs had purchased a new four wheel drive all-terrain Honda the month before in hopes of lessening the pulling and moving burden of their life on Humpback. Frank and Cindy, Wilbur, the school teacher, Ol' Gus and Aunt Bess all had a four-wheeler. Tad got tired of borrowing from the others each time he had a land project too big for his body to handle. He started the machine and swung it around and down to the water's edge.

"Bring me the gold line, Beth," Tad hollered. "Pull it clear of the boat."

Beth knew which one he meant right away. It was attached

to the tow line that pulled the logs. She unraveled it as she ran up the dock to Tad and the four-wheeler. Tad tied it with a set noose knot securely to the ball on the machine's hitch.

"Get on the four-wheeler and give it a pull up the beach till I say when," Tad instructed.

As Beth moved the machine the logs followed. When the logs hit the shoreline, Tad yelled, "Stop!"

Above high water, Tad had driven a pole deep into the beach sand. He tied the logs off securely while Beth pulled the noose from the ball hitch. Beth returned to Tad's side.

"Lets call it a day, honey," Beth suggested. "Can I get you a beer from the boat?"

"Sure, and pull the door tight. We'll leave it there for the night," Tad answered. "The tide will be out in the morning and I'll start bucking it up. We better get the boat out of the way before somebody screams about tying up all the dock space.

Upon arrival at their home, Beth felt something amiss. She walked to the side of the house. Her clothes line was twisted on the ground. A pole was down. Actually, a half of a pole was down. The other half still stuck out of the ground at a slight angle. "Tad," she called. "Tad..."

Tad walked around the corner with beer in hand. "For heaven's sakes," he exclaimed. "What in the hell happened here?"

Beth stood with her hands on her hips. "There must be a bear around," she said, with a guess that maybe one swam over from the mainland or Point Adolphus. Then she noticed the bucketful of water.

Tad saw the bucket at the same time. Then he noticed clear hoof prints in the grass and sand.

"Wait a minute—there's been a critter around, a moose or a cow or something."

Beth slapped her hands together in revelation. "Oh my gosh," she mumbled in a low voice. "Ah...Tad, honey, I kind of ordered you a surprise."

"Real nice, Beth—the damned yard is torn up," Tad replied.

Beth tramped around the site with her hands on her hips, taking in full gasps of air, exhaling as if she was blowing up a balloon. "Remember that fight we had? You know, the strawberry pie, the coffee, uh...the cow you kept saying I was having?"

Behind them through the alder bushes came a noise of someone moving. Norm pushed through the tangle of branches several feet from the usual trail.

"Oh, hi, Chief," Tad greeted. "What are you doing crawling through the bushes? You haven't joined up with the Park Service again, have you?"

"No, no," Norm replied. "I was here with the...the..." Norm looked around the disheveled yard. His face squished into an obvious perplexed expression. "Uh...well, I left my gloves on that stump."

Fisherman Frank and Cindy surprised the trio from behind, having walked around from the front of the house. "What's the occasion, gang?" Cindy said.

Frank stepped forward to see if he could see what the focus of everybody's attention could be. "You guys building a new clothesline?" he asked. "Nice load of wood down at the dock, Tad. Where did you get it?"

"Are you okay, Beth?" Norm asked, ignoring Frank's questions. Beth had turned pale. Her mouth open, she continued to suck air. Norm spotted his gloves and moved to pick them up inconspicuously.

"I think we have a problem, Frank," Tad remarked.

"Okay, Beth...Norm, what's the big secret here?"

Norm looked at Beth. Everybody had temporarily lost their ability to speak, expecting the other to come out with a clue.

Tad broke the nervous silence. "I think there's a cow on

the loose." He glanced at Beth for a confirmation. She whooshed a bellow of air from her lungs. Her facial color came rushing back like a dam of blood had burst loose from her throat.

"Yeah, I think you're right there," Norm quickly agreed. I helped bring a cow up here from the dock with this guy Clay from Hoonah. We tied it to your uh...post."

Cindy jumped with excitement. "A cow? Wonderful!" she exclaimed. "We came to invite everybody to a winter dance; you know, welcome in the cold and dark with a wild party or something. But to hell with that. Let's go find the cow. Whose idea was a cow?"

"I guess it was mine," Beth admitted. "I got it for Tad— sort of a joke. You know, Cindy, we had this fight and he...well, he kept saying I was having a cow." Beth glanced at Cindy for moral support. But Cindy wasn't paying attention; she was busy looking for a clue, a track. Frank was laughing. Norm helped Cindy with her tracking.

"Here they are, over here," Norm announced. "It went down this trail." Norm pushed through the alders a few feet to the side of where he came through in search of his gloves. Frank, Tad, and Cindy followed him immediately.

Beth broke out in tears and followed the rest of them sniveling. "Now I've gone and done it..." she muttered. She wiped her eyes with the sleeve of her sweatshirt.

The hoof prints trailed to the north up a slight incline toward the island's hump. New alder and willow, now without most of their leaves, created a maze for the trackers. Frank found a fresh cow pie amidst broken branches. It reminded him now of the day Tad wouldn't talk on the radio, Beth's unexplained trip. "Now I get it," Frank said aloud.

Tad overheard Frank's words. He followed right behind Frank. Norm forged ahead with his keen ranger skills.

"Get what?" Tad asked.

"Oh, nothing. I just put two and two together to make a cow," Frank answered. He laughed. "I can hear it now. 'You're having a cow,' right?" Frank slapped Tad in the arm with the back of his hand.

"I guess, maybe," Tad admitted and let out an embarrassed chuckle.

The search party emerged into a small clearing. They had paralleled one of Humpback's main thoroughfares, the trail to Aunt Bess's cabin. Wood smoke lifted from her metal chimney. Bess stepped from her door wearing a blue-checked apron and a wide grin. "I was just thinking how nice it would be to have some company. I have a fresh batch of cinnamon rolls on," Bess greeted.

"Have you seen the cow?" Norm asked.

"A cow?" Bess replied. She wiped her hands on the well-stained apron.

"We lost our cow," Tad reported.

"Well, now, that's interesting news. No, I haven't seen any stray cows today," Aunt Bess replied. She spurted a quick guffaw. "How about a hot roll and some coffee."

Beth piped up, "I'm getting cold. Do you have any hard stuff hiding in that secret cabinet of yours?"

"I have some homemade cranberry liqueur," Bess replied.

"Great, I'll have some," Beth accepted and stepped up on Bess's porch.

"Me, too," Cindy said, and followed Beth into the warmth of Aunt Bess's kitchen.

Tad and Frank bowed out of the cozy offer, Frank reminding Cindy to tell Bess about the dance. The three men continued on the trail of the cow tracks, Norm in the lead. The tracks lead past the side of the cabin, down the middle of the trail to Norm's place.

The afternoon slipped into evening with darkness closing in. The dark line of the storm from the south edged over the

Chilkat Mountains to the east and the high mountains on Chichagof Island to the southwest. The grey of night edged sooner than the sunset wanted. A breeze chilled the air. A winter chill felt imminent.

The three men quickened their pace. The cow's tracks pushed past Norm's new cabin. Clear plastic covered the windows. A door made from a plain piece of plywood covered the entry. "Looks like you have some work to do before the winter takes hold," Frank observed.

"Yeah. I don't know," Norm acknowledged. "Between lost cows and parties, I might have to button it up soon, lay on the beach in Mexico for the winter and get a fresh start come spring. I'm afraid I'm not as gung ho as I need to be."

They passed Norm's cabin and continued up the narrowing trail. A raven squealed at them from a young spruce tree. Tad pointed out another cow pie to the side of the trail. "We must be close," he declared.

"Yeah, I think I have a new neighbor," Norm mumbled.

Not far from the rear of Norm's cabin, just out of view, the side of a dark camouflage tent appeared. Norm stopped dead in his tracks. The sound of a cartridge being injected into a chamber jolted Frank and Tad to attention. Frank and Tad bumped against Norm. "Hold it," Norm said in a low voice. "I think we have a little problem here."

Before them in the near darkness stood a camouflaged figure. He held a shiny object...a gun. Behind him stood a brown and white cow.

"Excuse me, sir," Frank exhaled. "No need for a gun around here."

Tad pushed in front of the other two. "I think you have my cow. Who are you, anyway?"

Norm touched Tad on the arm to make him turn, if he would, and said in a hushed tone, "He's John. He came from Hoonah with the cow."

The stranger relaxed his grip on the gun. "My name's John, and I don't have your cow. It came here on its own. Real fine cow," he said, patting the cow's side. The gun was one-handed, then flipped to rest on John's shoulder.

"Do you plan on camping here?" Frank asked.

"Yes, I guess I do. Doesn't it look like it?" John replied.

Norm shook his head in frustration. Tad advanced to the cow, passing John en route. Norm and Frank relaxed when Tad had stepped around Weird John with no incident.

"Now what the hell am I ever going to do with a cow?" Tad asked.

"Two cows," John replied.

"What?" Tad exclaimed.

"The cow's going to calve" Norm piped in.

"Great," Tad declared. "So what am I going to do with two cows?"

"I like her. She's a nice cow," John argued. "What do you know about cows?" Tad asked.

"I was raised with cows in Colorado. I kind of miss 'em," John said. "I didn't know you had 'em here."

"Neither did I," Tad admitted.

Norm moved closer to the new neighbor. Frank followed behind. "Okay, guys, it's getting dark," Norm said. "How about we let John here keep a look out for the cow and we call it a day. The cow isn't going to get very lost on this little island. Okay, Tad?"

"If it was up to me, he could keep it," Tad answered. "But it's not. Beth bought the stupid cow."

"It's not a stupid cow. Anyway, you figure it out and let me know," John said. "I've got to finish putting my camp together. The cow came here on her own and she can stay here as long as she wants." John leaned his gun against the tent and went about unloading one of his duffel bags. Several boxes of ammo came out first.

Frank noticed the unusual supply of gun-related items. "Why all the guns?" he asked.

"Don't you have guns?" John replied. He continued to unload his bag.

Frank didn't have a reply other than, "Yes." He shrugged, turned to Norm and Tad and said, "Come on, guys, let's call it a night. The cow can stay here for now. Oh, by the way, John, we're having a dance tomorrow night at my place. Come if you want."

John didn't show any sign of acknowledging the invitation.

Norm, Tad, and Frank left the new settler and the cow with no more words exchanged.

Back at Aunt Bess's cabin, Beth had told Aunt Bess and Cindy her cow story over warm liqueur. The women laughed till their breath was gone and their bellies ached.

"Now what are you going to do with it?" Cindy asked.

"I don't know," Beth replied. "And there's two of them. She's pregnant. I can just see me out there milking cows every morning...yuch!"

Bess laughed again and then abruptly stopped. "I have an idea. Why don't we share the cow—cows?" she suggested. "You know, like a cow co-op or something."

Bright lights came on in their eyes. They poured another round of warm cranberry liqueur.

By the time the men returned, the women had a solid crimson color in their faces. Tad and Frank could hear them laughing from a couple hundred yards off and wondered whether to head home without them. Norm heard the commotion and bowed out at the turn to his cabin. "I'll let you husbands handle this," he said.

"Hi, guys," Cindy hollered when Tad and Frank opened the door. "Where's our cow?"

"Our cow?" Tad asked.

"The co-op cow, you know?" Aunt Bess replied. "I think it

might be Weird John's cow for now," Frank said.

"Weird John?" Cindy questioned.

"We found the cow up behind Norm's place in the high grass clearing. The critter seemed to be keeping this strange camouflaged fellow company," Tad replied. "Norm said he came on the Hoonah barge with the cow. He's got a tent set up and an arsenal plenty enough to attack Fort Knox."

"All sorts of news today," Beth remarked.

Frank found two cups in the cupboard. He poured hot water from the wood stove and then topped it off with Aunt Bess's famous cranberry liqueur. "We invited the guy to the dance. Hope he doesn't bring his weaponry," he said.

The next night, most everybody on the island showed up at Frank and Cindy's ready for a party. The storm that kicked up the night before brought warm rain. When people arrived, the evening was unusually warm and the rain had ceased about mid-afternoon. It was hard to tell from the weather that November would come in a few days, that Halloween would be the next festivity.

Cindy had thought to tell most everyone to bring something to munch on. What arrived was a ten course dinner from Alaska's finest home cooking. Darlene brought pickled kelp. Bess brought homemade bread and strawberry preserves. Tad and Beth brought smoked salmon. So did Frank. Ranger Norm came with instant pudding and graham crackers. And Ol' Gus managed three bags of tortilla chips and a secret recipe crab dip that he wouldn't confess the ingredients to no matter how much he was flattered.

The dance music came from Frank's battery-operated super boom box; the music—old rock 'n roll tunes from the Doors to the Boss, from the Supremes to the latest Rolling Stones and Eric Clapton.

When the pitch was feverish to the sound of Credence Clearwater, in walked Weird John. He stood by the door for the rest of the night, counting a perfect rhythm with his black-booted foot. He never cracked a smile nor uttered a word and nobody cared to push him.

Along about midnight, Cindy stopped the music and asked if anyone wanted some air. The house was so hot from human heat that it would take a week to cool off. Cindy grabbed a beer from the cooler and led the way.

She pushed past Weird John, who turned to follow her out the door. Standing in the front yard of Humpback's first house was none other than the island's first and only cow.

"She followed me," John announced.

"Wow," Cindy exclaimed, "Isn't she just wonderful?"

"Guess so," John replied.

Somebody found an old Jefferson Airplane tape and the party resumed. But the dancing spilled over to the porch and then the front yard. Aunt Bess, with an attempt to salvage the remains of her ear drums, joined Cindy and Weird John with the cow. Unable to stop the incessant rhythm inside her, Bess danced a lick with the cow. Cindy spotted Weird John trying to hide his smile. He discovered he'd been caught and said, "Yup, she's a real nice cow."

The clouds cleared away that night and the stars came out. A winter chill seized the dark and a hazy ground fog developed. About two in the morning when everybody realized the food was mostly gone and their feet had certainly had enough, the Northern Lights danced across the sky to light the way home. Norm walked with Weird John and the cow trailed along.

"It feels like winter's coming," Norm said to break the walk's silence.

John hesitated for the longest time and glanced from the cow to the sky. He put his hand into his camouflage pocket and retrieved a rolled marijuana cigarette. A Zippo lighter snapped and he took in a deep breath. Exhaling he said, "Yup, looks like."

Chapter 8

A Villain Visits

LIFE ON AN ISLAND THE SHAPE OF A HUMPBACK whale somewhere in the middle of Icy Strait, Alaska with only a handful or two of neighbors can have its low points. One of the testier times can come about when there's a newcomer. Accommodating a stranger in such a tiny social arrangement may upset the fragile fabric of things.

Without really trying, the folks of an isolated small town seem to develop a kind of outback or "cowboy's code" of getting along. People try not to mess with each other in certain ways in order to survive the isolation. Transgressions among insiders are often accommodated in some way. On the other hand, a social violation by an outsider is another thing.

Back in the time of the Old West, legends were written about the handsome stranger who came to town. He wooed and dazzled all the wives and daughters and was inevitably either strung up by his neck or run out of town at gunpoint by husbands and fathers. "He was a ranger and a rover and he meant no good." Little has changed in the New Northwest.

A stranger to an outback community may not be savvy to the local code either by ignorance or rebellious choice. Not everyone who happens on the social network of a small Alaskan community has the need or the desire to keep things the way they are. The stranger can blend into the social fabric by agreeing to the code or become a real pain by bringing his own needs to bear regardless. In some instances the villain breaks the rules because he has to—it is his style; he knows no other way. Those that he hurts have no meaning or bearing on him. If his neck is still attached, he moves on to the next small town to break another code.

Not long ago, soon after Humpback Island was first settled, the State Lands Department sent out a team of surveyors to study and mark the new island and much of the area around it. To transport the surveyors came a lone helicopter pilot. Buck, lean and handsome as he was, dressed more smartly than the local men, and talked of far loftier events and places than most of the Island's people could recently imagine.

Buck, being introduced around by his friend Bess, began by being nice to everyone. He was witty and quite personable. Late one fall, after having met Beth Neff in Hoonah, he returned to offer free rides for her and then eventually to other of the island people in his helicopter. He often brought from town beer for the men and fine wine for the women. "When I grow up," said the kids, "I want to be a helicopter pilot just like he is."

As time went on, however, it was the women who admired him most, and over his winter absence, his reputation flourished. It was the wives and daughters he spoke softly to and flattered with the mastery of his verbal magic. The helicopter rides had been designed to swirl and mesmerize. He showed up at every dance and community social gathering. As more time went on, the men lost their particular interest in the stranger and his helicopter and went back to their other pastimes.

After a winter and then again a spring, the pilot returned with his surveyors. By midsummer the field of Humpback Island women had been narrowed to three. After survey hours the helicopter buzzed overhead with the stranger's prey. Two women were married and the other was single.

Buck would lift them over mountaintops and land them on cliffs. His flattery was endless and his timing near perfect. His only flaw was his consistency, as he promised each of them the same thing.

For a time on our small island the men became more testy, fishing longer hours and consuming more beer at the dock. They talked of times when they were single and younger. Wild stories and beer made the men rowdy before heading home at night. The women blamed this on character defects in their men and the evils of alcohol.

The women began to wear more makeup and fixed their hair in something other than the usual scarf or ponytail. The odd smell of perfume drifted through the evening breezes. The men dismissed this fancy female vanity on the women's boredom or the effects of aging.

Only two of our locals avoided the helicopter and its handsome pilot. Ol' Gus said he was too old for the noise. Aunt Bess let it be known that she forgot how to flirt for favors. Gus told Bess at their usual meeting site, the post office, that "trouble was whirly-gigging around town." Bess winked in agreement. One evening Beth, knowing her husband had gone fishing, dressed real nice, put on some perfume, and went to the chopper's landing site. She waited for Buck's return from the day of surveying. When it finally arrived, Buck was not alone. Cindy was Buck's co-pilot, not the expected crew of tired surveyors. Cindy emerged from the cockpit exhilarated and laughing, one arm attached to Buck's, the other holding a bunch of high meadow wild flowers.

At first the women ignored each other. Beth knelt and pretended to search for berries as if she had another reason for being there. She picked a strawberry or two and ate them.

When Cindy realized it was Beth who watched her from the field, she detached her arm from Buck's and attempted to look more serious, as if she was on a business trip and had chartered Buck for the important mission. She stopped twenty feet from Beth.

Beth looked up at Cindy. Then they stared at each other. Buck discreetly ignored them with an about face to the helicopter.

After a long moment of silence, the two neighbors and friends laughed with each other. Neither of them said good-bye to Buck as he fiddled with his fancy machine. Walking towards their cabins, a third female friend made her way down the trail to the clearing. Beth and Cindy winked and waited until they heard the engine of the helicopter. The two friends then laughed in foolish embarrassment.

"What does he say to you?" Cindy asked.

"He offered to take me away from this little island," Beth replied. "He said I was the most special, that my beauty was rare."

"That your beauty was rare?" Cindy questioned with a hearty laugh. "That my beauty was rare," she said again and laughed at herself. "God, some stupid line, isn't it? At least he could try some variations."

They vowed to each other to not be so gullible and walked together with relief to the dock to look for their husbands.

That night, Cindy told Frank about her helicopter wanderings. Frank realized that he had been upset about something but he didn't know what. They laughed at each other's naive blindness.

Beth told Aunt Bess about the event. "I guess I had to take a look around a little bit once in a while to find out how good I have it. Tad is a good man, you know. I have to learn to keep a lid on my grass-might be-greener-thing.

Bess laughed. "I remember the first Park ranger ever to come to Glacier Bay. I was twenty-one. There were four of us in his dandy pocket until we ran him out of Gustavus. He was telling all four of us that he loved us and wanted to have babies."

With the summer's end and the survey completed, the helicopter left Humpback Island on schedule. The stranger was not alone for the flight. The unattached woman, one of the final three, went along for a while. But within a few weeks, she returned to the island with stories of Buck's wandering habits, the likes of which she swore she had never before seen.

In the weeks after the pilot left, the women wore less makeup, the men forgot all about it, and the children decided they really wanted to be fishermen when they grew up.

Chapter 9

Technology

MANY YEARS WENT BY ON OUR LITTLE ISLAND
before telephones, electricity, and television graced the lifestyle.
Home generators, battery operated radios, marine radios and
CBs, kerosene and propane lights, and a few lucky neighbors
with diesel generation were the best we could do. Some of us
spent a great deal of time researching and experimenting with
simply amazing homemade comfort devices.

One of everyone's favorite neighbors had just about everything a barnyard inventor could dream up to be comfortable on
a remote site. His backyard was a paradise of parts, previously
intended for or used on some brainstorm or another. Each and
every magical section of iron or unmatched bolt and nut waited,
patiently rusting, for the next symphony of handyman brilliance.

Ol' Gus, now eighty-something years old, refused to hook
up to anything like commercial power or television. He figured
that if he took part in the hysteria for modern convenience, he
wouldn't have a darned thing left to do, and his yard would
cease to be the community spare parts museum. His favorite
social event was to look for a neighbor's essential item among the
boxes and piles, serve up a round of black coffee, and hang on for
hours with the latest political gossip. A trip to Gus's parts museum had to be planned as a day's event.

At one time, Gus had three working gas and diesel generators, a windmill generator and a handmade pelton wheel in a
homemade creek. His electrical control panel, extension cord
nest and internal network of wires and boxes looked more like a

pop art masterpiece. The radio communications tower emitting from his kitchen window, on up his homemade gutter to the peak of his roof, could solicit the likes of the Guinness editorial staff. Somehow or another, he converted his refrigerator into a working power antenna for a sideband radio. He often spent his Saturday nights discussing world politics with someone in Iceland or Siberia.

Not surprisingly, there have been times in the social history of our handyman's paradise when community decisions had to be made as to whether or not to allow a wholesale introduction of a new technological convenience. Some residents had resented and resisted any change. Some see a new convenience more of a reason to stay. Entrepreneurs recognize a possibility of added income, and with each new convenience comes a new family or two in island population.

The most memorable and hotly debated community question I can recall was whether or not to allow the State of Alaska to provide the island with free television. On his own, Tad Neff approached the State with the possibility of putting in a satellite dish. Needless to say, others had a difference of opinion. The debate went on for months and a few friendships were sorely tested. Sided arguments went something like this:

"Our kids will be ruined. T.V. makes children become lazy and dull, and their eyesight will be wrecked."

"The women will stay home all day watching soap operas and game shows. Nothing will get done."

"All he'll ever do on weekends is watch football. My new kitchen won't ever get finished."

"I don't own a television and I'll be darned if they're going to make me."

"So what if they put in a satellite dish? Who's going to pay to maintain it?"

"I have my own satellite dish. It's not my problem. I'd just as soon not have to pay for another. If they want one, let them buy one."

"Our children's perspectives will be broadened. Just think of the wonderful educational programs and news of major events."

After weeks of community discussion and Thursday night association meetings, the Island Volunteer Ad Hoc Committee decided to bring the satellite dish to a vote. In the first referendum, the pros and the cons deadlocked in a tie. Wives voted against husbands, uncles and aunts voted against their nephews and nieces. Everybody canceled out everybody else's vote. On the day of the ballot, Ol' Gus drove an ATV around on the beach with a banner and a loud speaker. A recorded message repeated, "Doom is soon if you vote for a cartoon." The banner read, "Vote NO DISH!"

In the second ballot, the person who volunteered to be in charge, Darlene, mysteriously deleted twenty of the eligible voters' names in her mail-out. The missing page was found in her daughter's Sesame Street lunch box. The girl used the voting list to catch the juice from peeling an orange for school snack time. The teacher discovered it when the kid started reading the names out loud in between orange slices.

In the third vote, only forty of the possible eighty neighbors voted. A sizeable number of island voters had left for their winter holiday. A disgruntled loser challenged the validity of the vote, and in the spirit of friendship and fairness, the new volunteer election official, Beth Neff, scheduled another referendum at a time when most everybody would be present.

In the meantime, the State Telecommunications Office sent a letter to the postmaster and indefinitely delayed installation of the satellite due to recent budget shortfalls.

Frank and Cindy, Gus's closest neighbors, were one of the divided households. Cindy thought television was going to be the ruination of their lifestyle. Frank wanted to watch the statewide weather and the news. When the State sent the letter of postponement, Frank secretly took the cause on and called his state representative. He never told Cindy that he was the one responsible for the representative getting a special capital improvement grant to fund the island's dish.

Finally, after several months of anticipation, arguments, and a certain wedge between all the philosophical factions of our community, the television issue won acceptance. Only 63 people voted. The final count was 31 against and 32 for.

Today, most people have multiple television sets. Only Ol' Gus remains without. Nevertheless, he unfailingly watches the "The Price is Right" each and every day at his nephew's house and the Alaska weather at his closest neighbor's. "The Price is Right" comes on during lunch. The state weather, of course, is at dinner. Gus swears he pays his daily respects to be neighborly. But then, once his plate is full, try to pull him away from the evils of modern communication.

Chapter 10

Newcomers

EVERYTHING WENT REASONABLY WELL FOR THE Humpback Islanders for several years. After Frank and Cindy set up their first little camp, there came a smattering of independent-minded homesteaders seeking a better variation from the life they had known elsewhere.

Like Frank and Cindy, many of them came to the island via the booming community of Gustavus. Others just happened along. The universal draw seemed to unanimously be the abundant wildlife and natural quiet. Folks sought freedom from artificial rules and restrictions, traffic, congested shopping malls and the fear of violent crime.

Some fished for a living. Some were either retired from the Park Service or commuted by skiff to work in Bartlett Cove. Many were retired or wealthy from endeavors in the city. Some were poor and knew how to get by.

The unsaid belief was that the island was small enough and the people unique enough that one could keep track of destiny. A person could walk the perimeter of the planet, so to speak, in one leisurely day. A neighbor knew every other neighbor's birthday, wedding anniversary, and state of health. Your neighbor's visiting relatives were on a first-name basis.

But the wildlife was so darned plentiful and the fishing and hunting so superb that to keep it all a secret from outdoor fun-seekers became plain impossible. With the national park just a stone's throw away, the island became a sitting duck for international tourism.

For a long time the hold-up for the pending onslaught of tourists resulted from the economic fact that there were no properties for sale and no places to stay other than Frank and Cindy's spare room, another islander's floor, or a tent. The homesteaders refrained from the temptation to own or, heaven forbid, sell their land. Nobody had title to land on Humpback Island. The State wanted it, the Park Service wanted it, the rich folks wanted it, Dan-Hank-Bert-Jack each thought they had an explorer's claim on it. Various other special interest groups wanted it. The nightmare legal battle for the island's land was the immediate blessing. Land ownership was indefinitely tied up in the courts.

Then one summer a retired cruise ship captain from San Diego, California with a cantankerous vision for the new island happened along. In a dense fog, Captain San Diego and a bunch of his slightly inebriated cronies from California ran aground on the western side of the Island. Fishing on a chartered boat from Juneau owned and piloted by the "tricka-tricka" biologist, Brad Stewart, the guys were having so much fun they lost track of their course. High and dry on the beach till the next flood tide, they decided to disembark for a look around.

Nobody lived on the western side of the island for no particular reason. Homesteads were built on the other side of the hump because that's where the first explorers landed and that's where Frank and Cindy started the first shack. The islanders used the western side as sort of a free zone; a place to walk and fish and hunt and watch the sunset. Aunt Bess had a secret berry patch there. Ol' Gus had a favorite goose hunting blind even though he rarely hunted and everybody else used it without letting on.

Upon their return to the charter boat, Captain San Diego decided then and there that he was going to build a hotel and fishing dock right where the boat sat stuck on a rock. His buddies thought he was out of his mind.

"I knew you were crazy, ya old sea shark," said one.

"Hell, ya can't even drive a damned boat," said another. They all laughed.

"I'll bet each of you fools a thousand-dollar bill that I'll do it," said the captain as he turned, unzipped and drained the beer over the port side. "Put your money where your ugly drunk mugs are, ya' silly light-weights," he said again, as he leaned over to zip up. He turned back to his audience, smiled triumphantly, and boasted, "It'll be done by next fall."

"You're mental, but you're on, captain," said the drunkest mate and they all eventually agreed to the challenge.

On schedule with the bet, early the next spring a dilapidated barge from Seattle delivered eight double-wide trailers to the spot. The same day a dozen Spanish-American laborers flew in by floatplane. In a month's time there was a hotel that looked like a distorted logging camp, a plywood dock, three sport fish vessels, and a vessel owned by none other than Brad Stewart that looked a lot like a small version of a big time, ocean-going fish processing boat; the vessels name—the "F.V. Pacific Tricka-Tricka."

Aunt Bess hadn't heard a word about it. When she figured the first of her secret strawberries were ripe, she hiked the few miles to the western side of the island just as she had done for who knows how long. As she rounded the last shoal before her patch, she saw the mess, gasped, and fainted dead away on a soft sandy spot.

Two of the captain's construction crew, each capable of speaking predominantly Spanish, found Bess spread-eagle on the sand. They carried her gently to the office trailer and hollered for the boss. "Hey Capitan," they yelled. "We fown thees ol' girl on thee sand. Maybe she hass a heart eettack or somethin."

The captain and his wife nursed her back to consciousness, helped her to her house and said, "Come back when you're feeling better."

"*My Gawd*, Cindy," Bess cried upon her breathless return

home. Within moments, she was on Cindy's doorstep yelling, "They've invaded us. They've ruined our island!"

"Who? what?" asked Cindy, trying to be as calm as she could be.

"I don't know. I just can't believe it. There's a great big trailer house over there in my secret berry patch with some sort of toy dock and a bunch of boats. And a big fishing boat of some sort. They can't do that!"

"Frank said there was a barge anchored off over there about a month ago," Cindy remembered. "Guess I thought it was headed out to a logging camp or something."

"Now what'll we do?" Bess asked. She felt a little better knowing it was a shared concern. "You got any of that cranberry liqueur? I could use a little pick-me-up."

Cindy ignored her request and proceeded to think out loud. "What we need is to call a meeting. We had better bring this up at an emergency session of the Island Association."

"I still think my heart could use a little slow- down, honey," Bess tried to interrupt, "at least before we get all bothered over one of those darn meetings again. My whistle could use a little wettin'."

"Better try to raise Frank on the radio," Cindy said, continuing to be oblivious to Bess's request.

"Remember that meeting we had about whether the ferries should come here?" Bess asked. "I thought nobody would say a word to nobody ever again. It was almost three days till you could set foot in the post office without fearing for your life."

Cindy got up and grabbed the marine radio microphone off the wall. Bess went through the plywood cupboards until she found what she wanted—a mason jar full of crimson liquid.

Bess found a cup and poured a small amount. "Nice batch," Bess exhaled. She proceeded to pour a slightly larger quantity.

"Want to switch to channel ten?" Cindy asked Frank.

"Frank, what's going on over there on the west side? How come you guys haven't said anything about it? Aunt Bess just had the shock of her life over there when she found those trailers. Are they permanent? Over..."

"Looks like, dear," Frank replied. He clicked the microphone to let her know he was finished with his come-back. He seemed purposely brief.

"Now, come on, Frank, what in the hell is happening over there? Over."

"Not much we can do about it," Frank said, contradicting Cindy's urgent tone. "The guy has as much right to it as we do."

"It sounds like he's your best buddy, Frank. I suppose you and all the other guys have been stopping in there and have been getting all buddy-buddy over a new stash of beer. Who is this *guy* you're talking about, anyway?" Cindy yelled.

"Just some guy and his wife from California. Seemed like sort of an eccentric sort of character, but they're nice enough. Guess he's going to try to run a few sport fishing boats, try to catch some little Japanese delicacy called a tricka-tricka fish, and bring his friends in for a good time in the wilderness. Not a whole lot we can say about it."

"But what gives him the right to just show up out of nowhere? What's the matter with you, Frank?" Cindy screamed through the radio. She had a head of steam up now. "You want this place to look like San Diego? Why in the hell did they come here, anyway?"

"Funny you should say that, Cindy," Frank answered calmly. "That's what they call him—Captain San Diego. Ha! And he calls the place he's going to build the '*Wayindaheyda Conifer Resort!*' Over."

Aunt Bess laughed hysterically at the resort's name. All the while listening to the radio conversation, Bess drank her homemade liqueur. As she became more relaxed, Cindy grew more excited.

"Okay, that's it," Cindy said. "We're having a meeting to-morrow night. And you better tell all your friends out there fishing that it's an important one. Over and *Out!*" She hung up the microphone and turned off the radio.

"Captain San Diego? My Gawd," Cindy mumbled. "Why in the hell did he come here, anyway?"

Bess doubled over in stitches. "Why in the hell did ya come here resort! That's about as good as Ya-all Come Back Saloon...or the Rest in Peace Inn—that's where we held my uncle's funeral down in Montana." Bess couldn't stop. "Ha! Captain San Diego."

Cindy sat down for a glass of liqueur. She wasn't amused. She was steaming.

The island meetings were held next to Frank and Cindy's original shack. A one-room schoolhouse built by the district was the location for about everything from bingo to national elections. The shack was now the post office and telephone booth. A view of Gustavus dock was straight across the water to the east.

Just about everybody came to this particular meeting. Either it was a hot issue or there was not much else going on that night. Gus, who never liked meetings and rarely attended, came dressed as usual in his farmer's blue overalls, covered with grease or soot or something black from the day's project. Weird John came dressed in his camouflage suit with a ten inch black blade on his belt and red bandanna tied floppily on his head. Debbie brought all her three kids and sat in the front. Frank had noti-fied the island's fishing fleet and most all of them showed up. With babies, kids, summer visitors, and relatives, it was standing room only in the little school house.

Aunt Bess was a board member. Cindy was the treasurer and Ranger Norm, retired, the current chairman of the board. Norm called the meeting to order by tapping his coffee cup on the shipping pallet table set on sawhorses.

"Okay, okay, everybody. Let's get a move on here. Does

anybody want to hear the minutes from the last meeting?"

Nobody said a word. Somebody burped.

"Well, does anybody want to bring up any old business?"

Again there was silence, except one of Debbie's kids said, "Look at the hair coming out of his nose." She pointed at Gus's nose, and the whole room turned to look. Gus pretended not to notice.

"Guess we can move on to the new stuff," Norm went on. "Cindy, here, kind of called this emergency meeting to discuss the development on the western side of our island. Now, personally, I think we ought to invite this Captain San Francisco guy and his wife over to meet us. On that note, I'll open it up to discussion. Cindy, since you initiated this, you start us up."

Norm pointed at Cindy. She looked around to make sure nobody would complain and stood up. Frank, sitting next to Cindy, covered his eyes with his hand as though there was bright sun in the room. Then he crossed his legs and put his right elbow on his highest crossed leg.

"Ahhem," Cindy started. "It seems to me that we have a new situation on our island. Up until now everybody who has come to live here has done so with the idea that they want our island community to be unique. We don't have tourist traps or motels or fancy things to make life easy. We don't own our land nor do we want anybody to get greedy at the expense of the rest of us. Sure, we don't have any real laws or zoning requirements. There are no rules or restrictions, as long as you don't hurt somebody or intrude on somebody else's space."

Cindy glanced around the room. Gus had his eyes closed and his chin resting on his chest. Aunt Bess looked like she wanted to say something. Frank had removed his hands from his eyes, uncrossed his legs and was looking at her approvingly. Debbie's mother, Dehlia, was fidgeting in her chair. The kids were listening for a change. Cindy had mysteriously gained their attention.

"Well," Cindy continued, "this newcomer, ah…Captain San Diego, came here with no idea what we are all about. Without even saying boo to any of us he put a bunch of ugly trailers on Bess's secret berry patch." Everybody in the room smiled and glanced down. Bess didn't notice, but "hrrrumphed" and set her arms like that of a chief in disgust. "Let me remind you, since this island has limited space and because it's so new, there is only one other spot that has any berries. And that's not a secret," she said. She started to get heated up.

"Now, if we let this happen, what's to stop other people from doing it? Then we'll be just like Gustavus or Juneau or West Yellowstone, won't we? Next thing you know we'll have a Holiday Inn on the north side, and Glacier Bay Motel and Resort on the south side, and nobody will have room to park their boats!" Cindy was cookin' now—her voice cracked and her hands flailed in animation.

Frank had his hand over his eyes again. Cindy continued to stand and appeared to not be finished.

Weird John stood up abruptly from his crouch on the floor near the door at the back of the room. His eyes were typically glazed. With his voice low and deep, he said, "Let me take care of the sucker."

Norm reacted with embarrassment. His face turned ashen, splotched with red. He looked around the room and cleared his throat, "Ahhem, anyone else?"

Weird John stood at attention for several seconds; one hand on his long black knife. His expression did not change. His glassed glare focused ahead into space. Cindy, in frustration, sat down.

Jimmie, a balding, tall and skinny fisherman, a friend of Frank's, who talked his wife into selling a nice house in Sitka to move to Humpback Island, raised his hand. Everybody was sort of surprised. Jimmie rarely spoke at these meetings, although he could jawbone your ear off on a sunny afternoon on the water.

Jimmie's wife, Sara, a husky woman, had the only real gift of public speech in the family. A part-time teacher's aide, weekend babysitter, and island gossip, her best calling card was her fresh-baked bread. Sara tried to pull Jimmie's arm down but realized everybody saw her try do it and then she tried to hide her maneuver by patting his wrist. The crowd sighed in relief.

Cindy saw Jimmie's hand, looked at Norm and said, "Go ahead, Jimmie."

"You done, Cindy?" Norm asked.

"I guess for now," Cindy answered.

"Go for it, Jimmie," Norm said as he pointed his finger again.

Jimmie didn't stand up. "Whay'll, seems we have a real problem here. By golly, I don't like it any more than you do…ah…Cindy. But, what are we going to do about it?"

Sara whispered loudly, "Stand up, Jimmie. Stand up!" She punched him in the side with her elbow.

"Damn," Jimmie exhaled as he stood up and winced slightly in pain. He hunched over and leaned with two hands on the back of Debbie's chair. "But what are we going to do about it?" he asked again. "The guy is already moved in. You should see his water and power system; it must-a' cost him a bloody fortune. Don't care too much for his dock, though. It'll probably come apart in the first storm. Anyway, guess he has as much right to run around here on this lump of land as we do. I don't like it, though. It's going to make things different, for sure. If it gets too weird on this little island, I guess I can just pack it up again like we did in Sitka. That place used to be nice, too. But then there were the strikes at the mill and the chain motels moved in. Heck, I used to know everybody in Sitka, and now I hardly know anybody. Taxes got terrible, and the police couldn't keep up with the vandalism and juvenile delinquents." Jimmie's thoughts just sort of drifted off for a minute. His eyes rolled up and then back into place. He looked down.

"Oh, yeah," he remembered, "vandalism and robbery and stuff. Whay'll, guess that's all I wanted to say," he ended and looked at his wife. Sara shook her head.

Jimmie pushed off of Debbie's chair like he was doing a pushup. He sat down with a thunk.

Debbie's kids chased each other around Norm. He didn't pay any attention and asked, "Anybody else?"

From the back of the little room came a familiar voice at these meetings. "Yes, I'd like to say one thing."

"Okay, guess so," Norm answered from the chair-table. He didn't point his finger; he didn't need to. "Darlene, you have the floor."

Darlene stepped forward just enough to gain visual contact with most of the room. Everybody turned to look at her. She held the hand of a little girl that looked like a miniature replica of herself.

Darlene had become one of the most outspoken members of the community. Some say she was the smartest. A tall and large-boned woman, she was both pretty and muscular. Her hair was cut medium length and usually tied with a bandanna. Her clothes were the perfect mixture of carpenter, fisherman, and feminine-outdoor life. A successful commercial fisher-woman, scholar, artist, homemaker, journeyman carpenter, and top notch mechanic, she had one six-year-old female child who was very much the same.

Darlene was eight months pregnant when her husband, a successful fisherman, ran off with an eighteen-year-old he met in the Park Lodge bar and was killed in a freak accident a year later aboard a friend's boat. A few months later, her house burned to the ground in Gustavus. They say she could take on just about anything or anybody when it came to a challenge or a disaster. To her, Captain San Diego was nothing more than a fly on the surface of life.

"Is this a lynching mob or a welcoming committee?" she

asked. Darlene paused and looked around for emphasis. "I suggest you all remember what it was like when you first got here to Humpback Island. If the rules are different for these new people than they were for me, then I have no further business in this meeting." She stepped back one pace. Darlene had done it again.

After a long pause Norm asked, "Is there any more discussion on the matter?"

There was not a sound in the room for several long seconds. Tad finally stood up and said, "Yeah, I think Darlene's right." He sat back down. His wife Beth smiled approvingly.

"Any more?" Norm asked again. "Well, in that case, does anyone have any suggestions on where to go from here?"

"I do, ahhem," announced Aunt Bess, clearing her throat. "How about we invite them to a potluck? You know, check them out."

"Do you want to put that in the form of a motion?" Norm asked.

"Well, yes, I guess I do," Bess answered. "I make a motion that we invite the whole bunch of 'em over for a halibut fry and music. We can call it the Wayindaheydya Conifer jamboree— just for the halibut." Bess burst into another spontaneous round of laughter, slapping her knee repeatedly.

Norm pounded the table with his cup while trying to restrain his own laughter. "Okay, okay, everybody, there's a motion on the floor. Is there any discussion?"

Cindy stood up again. "I've just got one thing to say," she pleaded. "You all know that this is the beginning of something we can never undo. Maybe we can't stop it and maybe it was inevitable. But just remember for a moment what it was like here on this crazy little island yesterday before this happened to us. Remember when we fished and hunted over there on the western side. Remember the sunsets and the geese. Remember Aunt Bess's secret berry patch that everybody knew about."

Cindy started to cry. "Remember what it was like," she sobbed, and sat down. Frank covered his eyes again.

Bess's motion passed nineteen to seven. Norm tried to officially adjourn the meeting, but everybody started talking at once. He gave up and started talking, too.

A week later, Captain San Diego and his Juneau friend, Brad Stewart, provided the halibut, the beer, and the horseshoes for the now annual event. Bess brought her secret berry pie.

After a year of refusing to acknowledge the new resort existed at all, Cindy's best friend Beth went to work the following season for the Wayindaheydya Conifer Resort. She was the manager of the reservations and sport-fishing charters. A year later she convinced the Captain to sell his trailers and build a beautiful frame lodge.

To the immediate south of the lodge is the finest berry patch in Southeast Alaska, thanks to the loving care of Aunt Bess. Darlene was the foreman on the lodge construction project, along with Bert, the foreman in charge of moving the dirt, and they both took turns maintaining the all the heavy equipment. The fishermen, Jimmie, Tad, and Frank, supply all the fresh fish that is famously prepared in the lodge's kitchen. The bread chef, of course, is Jimmie's wife, Sara.

Early in the fall goose season after the Wayindaheydya Lodge had opened for its first full season of tourists, Gus took his old shotgun over to the tide flats just north of the lodge and shot off a box of shells. There were rarely any geese in that close to the lodge anymore. Ol' Gus continues this annual ritual and every now and again he breaks a window or two. Nobody knows whether it's a gesture of rebellion or just Gus's way to remember the old days.

Chapter 11

The School

WITH THE MINI-ONSLAUGHT OF IMMIGRATING homesteaders to the island came a whole new dimension to community accommodations. The first indication of change, although obscure, was the arrival of Jimmie and Sara with their four kids. Darlene moved over from Gustavus with her six-year-old. Shortly after, Debbie and her mother, Dehlia, moved in with Debbie's three daughters. Suddenly there were six school-age children and more on their way. At first, with only two or three little ones, it was assumed that school would be a matter of home and field education. As for Darlene and Debbie, the Bush method of education, home correspondence, would be just fine. Not for Sara; Sara expected more.

Jimmie and Sara had come from Sitka, a town known for its complete array of public education facilities. With a college, two high schools, and two elementary schools, not to mention a school-supported before-and-after hours public babysitting service, a swimming pool, and an array of gymnasiums, Sitka was a mother's dream. Sara had enjoyed the best of Alaska's educational system.

When Sara and Jimmie discussed the move from less desirable social amenities in a larger town to the romantic existence on a remote island, they neglected the school thing in their considerations. Not till the first September came along did Sara realize that her move to Humpback had one very big deficit. Nobody, except Sara, had considered it necessary to generate public education, a costly super bureaucracy thought by many island residents to be somewhat decadent, overgrown and useless. Sara, however, would not stop until her children had somewhere to call school, no matter who benefited from the six hours of respite. Those opposed did not put up much of a fuss until it was too late in the game.

So it went. Outspoken Sara called the island's state representative and senator, the State Department of Education and even the governor's office. Wa-la—Humpback Island had a school. Not just the one-room school for a handful of Bush kids put up by a smattering of carpenter-wise parents, but a big, architecturally awesome school with four classrooms, a multi-purpose room, an office, a library, and a playground; all for nine kids, half of whom were Sara's. Most others came reluctantly, the parents preferring to teach their kids how to gut salmon and change oil on a diesel backhoe.

With a real school came a paid teacher. Nobody knows how, but for some miraculous cosmic reason, the majority of parents lucked out. This first Humpback Island teacher, named Wilbur Cook, provided a Bush teacher's role model straight from the Gary Cooper/John Wayne school of teaching. Tall and handsomely rugged-looking, with a full beard and a knee-slapping sense of humor, he came to school most days wearing hip boots and a hunting vest covered with blood or feathers. When he happened to be otherwise occupied and therefore late from the field for the first bell, his wife Laura, a fully credentialed teacher on her own, would simply start the class and move over when the old man showed up.

Many a perfect hunting day would find the school children tramping through the knee-deep grass behind Wilbur learning a thing or two about nature. Some say that on one Tuesday morning, the class somehow bagged four mallards, two geese, a bagful of nagoonberrys, and three silver salmon. "See here," Mr. Wilbur would say, "this is very essential education. We have a responsibility to teach our children the wonders of their immediate environment." And he did, even if it meant slugging waist high through Hell-and-Gone Creek or across Blueberry Ridge.

Wilbur taught his students the flight patterns of geese, the depth of big halibut during a particular month of the year, and how to call in a Sitka Blacktail Deer with an alder leaf. It was Wilbur and the kids who spotted the first moose on the island and Wilbur and the kids who saved a baby deer from drowning.

One day I asked my daughter what she did in school. "Well, Dad," she explained, for P.E. we jogged to Humpy Creek. For math, we counted the geese at the mouth of Hell-and-Gone Creek. For spelling we had to spell the names of ducks, like M-A-L-L-A-R-D and P-I-N-T-A-I-L. Then for biology we identified the difference between willow and alder, gathered willow twigs, and made miniature duck blinds. For home economics we caught a bunch of salmon from the Humpy Creek with our hands by tickling them on their belly and then roasted the suckers right in the middle of the alder camp fire. Did you know that the skin of a fish is like tinfoil?" Now, not every parent got behind this down-to-earth kind of common sense approach to teaching. Especially when the kids didn't want to come home from school—they were having too much fun. And, you guessed it, Sara didn't see exactly eye-to-eye with Mr. Wilbur's methods of teaching the four R's—the fourth R standing for reel, as in fishing reel.

On the other hand, Sara's husband, Jimmie, felt rather different about the matter. He was a fisherman.

But Jimmie stayed out of it, as he usually did, in spite of Wilbur's call for help. Jimmie said, "I decide where we live and Sara takes charge of the kids." Sara originally came from Portland, Oregon. She didn't want her children to grow up, then spend their days in slime and bait. No, it must be college degrees and laundered clothes for her children, nothing else.

Within six months of the first school year for Wilbur and the first year in the new school, Sara had irritated the state officials enough to cause Wilbur to think that Humpback Island wasn't so friendly. Notwithstanding the fact that most of the island's parents thought Wilbur taught with great art and compassion, Sara was enough of an irritant to make a school day uncomfortable for everybody, especially when she began coming to school with her kids at the nine a.m. bell and refusing to leave until it was time for her nap at one-thirty.

Sara's help at school, while not wanted by anybody except Sara herself, put a definite crunch on creative outdoor learning events. The most obvious display of dissatisfaction came when the older boys began falling asleep in class. Sara insisted on a quiet reading hour from after lunch until she left at one-thirty. She believed this would give Wilbur a chance to prepare intellectually stimulating first and second grade lectures. The boys were so overwhelmingly bored, they fell asleep on their books. When Wilbur defiantly changed the after-lunch hour to P.E., Sara called the State Board of Education and dumped a whole load of pent-up "men shouldn't be allowed to teach elementary-isms." Unfortunately, the female State Board staffer she happened to be connected with on the phone didn't confess that her husband taught first grade. Whoops.

Suddenly there came a state rule that parents limit their school assistance to one hour per day. Sara steamed. At home, Jimmie again stayed out of it, except to sneak off with Wilbur for occasional winter king salmon fishing on the weekends.

On one of those "where is Jimmie" weekend days, Sara's oldest little genius, Jonathan, a third grader, tried to roast a marshmallow in the living room with the wood stove firebox door open. Somehow the marshmallow flamed, and Jonathan, in terror or just plain meanness, flipped the little flaming missile into the paper box. Before he noticed the inferno, he had already moved to the next project outside. Sara found herself evacuating the remaining kids, the keepsakes, and the encyclopedia before the new, undone house became a dazzling light show never before seen on the island.

When Jimmie returned to find only ash where the house had been, their neighbor Darlene let him know that Wilbur's wife, Laura, temporarily agreed to let his family move into the school for lack of anyplace else. When Wilbur later found out, he could only come out with two kind words for his wife's brainstorm of generosity. "Gee thanks, dear."

The island's first fire disaster became the reason for the island's first discussion of the need for some sort of volunteer fire and disaster team. Wouldn't you know who would be the leader in the community effort to form a volunteer fire department—Wilbur. "The first thing we need to do is help Jimmie and Sara build a new house," Wilbur announced at the Community Ad Hoc Volunteer Council meeting. "Then we need to prevent such a disaster from happening again."

At the first meeting, the island residents had to decide by majority vote how to spend the State Department of Community and Regional Affairs grant of $20,000.00 for fire related assistance. Roberts Rules expert, and voluntary president of the Council, retired ranger Norm, put the issue on the table. "Okay, everybody, we have some money for fire-related problems," he began. "Does anyone have an idea—or rather a motion on the issue of fire protection?"

Sara raised her hand. "I could have put that fire out if we had a fire extinguisher," she said.

Jimmie nudged his wife and whispered, "I have three on the boat, honey."

"Let me see by a show of hands who has a working fire extinguisher in their house," Norm asked.

Only Ol' Gus raised his hand. "I got burned out in fifty-two over in Gustavus," Gus informed. "I have one in every room."

"Does anyone have a comment about our seeming lack of fire preparedness?" Norm asked.

Debbie's mother, Dehlia, a widow on Social Security and forever complaining about money, raised her hand. "I do," she said. "How about we buy a nice fire extinguisher for everybody here? Then everybody on the island will be safe."

Never afraid to solve problems, Aunt Bess said, "I second that vote."

Gus added, "I could use one more in my outhouse."

"Any discussion on the motion?" Norm queried. "Yes, I do," Wilbur said. "I kind of thought we'd think about helping Jimmie and Sara build back up and maybe get a real community fire pump or something."

"Anybody else?" Norm inquired.

Aunt Bess, the peacemaker in the group, had a healthy mind when it came to social efforts. "Jimmie said his father in Sitka could help out with money for the house. Now, if we bought a fire pump, would it be more than, say, five thousand dollars? That would certainly leave us enough for the fire extinguishers and maybe even some good old-fashioned buckets and shovels too. I'm sure we can put together a work party, can't we?" Bess turned to the rest of her neighbors for a signal that they'd help.

Twelve cases of fire extinguishers arrived on the first spring barge, along with a $6,000.00 pump that could be carried on the back of a small pickup and then thrown in the water by two strong men for a quick stream of water. The shovels and buckets came by fishing boat not two weeks after the meeting and were put to immediate work when the community volunteer committee showed up to plant Jimmie and Sara's new foundation.

Jonathan, Sara's oldest, and to this day referred to as the "missile," took it upon himself to test the readiness of the shovel brigade by setting the grass on fire in the vicinity of the family's building site. The shovels did, in fact, work on the grass fire, but some believed they would be better put to use on Jonathan's hide. At least one thing was firmly decided by all other parents: "If you dare let your children play with Jonathan, be sure to give them a fire and hazard safety lecture first." Darlene went so far as to set up a schedule for all of Jonathan's playmates so they could take a supervised mercy turn with the dangerous "missile."

Norm, Frank, Tad, Jimmie, Darlene, and Wilbur formed the first volunteer Humpback Emergency Rescue Squad—HERS, as it's known today, partly from the team's initials and mostly due to the incredible efforts of Darlene, the best emergency medical technician in northern Southeast Alaska.

Wilbur went back to his style of teaching before the end of Jimmie and Sara's temporary residence at the schoolhouse. According to Wilbur, "She couldn't find a quiet place to take her naps. After a month of non-stop meddling in my teaching, Sara asked me to be sure to get the kids outside after lunch."

Chapter 12

Ducks & Freeways

ABOUT THE END OF SEPTEMBER, THE LAST SIGN OF visiting relatives and tourists disappear from Humpback Island. Migrating waterfowl replace the bikers, hikers, fisherpersons, and kayakers who have inhabited the beach waters and inner island creeks and sloughs. The alders and willows turn yellow and brown, then drop their leaves to reveal open landscapes forgotten from the winter before. Stocks of fireweed and lupine stand like corn in broad and yellowed fields. Days become dark afternoons and the rain falls heavier and longer, muddying the creeks and sloughs.

Braced for one more winter, islanders find time to enjoy the quiet and ponder the weather's next astounding turn. The summer fishing season draws to a close and the fleet returns home to make families complete. Firewood is cut, chopped, and stacked. Coho salmon fight to spawn in the creeks, making for the year's best fishing, while deer run for cover from the hunters on nearby islands. Alderwood smoke curls up from home-made smokehouses to preserve the last batch of salmon filets.

Wilbur, our one and only and multi-talented school teacher, retires his sport rods from a season of guiding and becomes the chief engineer of Humpback Island's social activities. Teaching navigation, biology, English, history, reading, and math in the same morning to a handful of different-aged students, Wilbur makes time afterwards to set his decoys on the north side creek between the tails of the Humpback. Rarely is he known to not leave a pile of feathers in the beach grass like a sentinel of his perfect adaptation to this remote wonderland. The duck blinds he made last year are museums of empty shot shells. Other hunters swear that the blinds are constructed of Wilbur's shells, his feathered prey's bones, and the glue of his spirited perseverance.

Another prominent outdoor enthusiast on Humpback Island was fisherman Frank. Born somewhere inland in the Rocky Mountains to a school-teacher mother and a fishing father, Frank learned from birth the fine balance of the water and had a distinct nose for wildlife. When he pushed out of high school, his parents insisted he use his faculties in college; at least give it a try. He tried and it didn't work.

Desiring a change from the attention of his parents, he moved north to Juneau and then Gustavus to be closer to the lucrative Icy Strait, Glacier Bay, and Cross Sound fishery. He rented a friend's guest cabin in Gustavus and then met Cindy on a halibut opening. With her, they became founders of the strange little Humpback Island settlement.

Through years of arguing, fishing, and gray afternoons in the fall rain, Frank and Wilbur became the very best friends. Some island folks say, "If it wasn't for the two of them, Humpback Island would be about as boring as a church on Wednesday."

One beautiful fall afternoon Frank and Wilbur were out on the Island Tails scoping out the geese population when they spotted a rare bull moose swimming to shore. Rather than shoot it, keep it quiet, and fill their freezers, the boys gathered everybody on the island for a look-see. When the moose started getting feisty and confused with all the attention, they navigated it back to the mainland with the help of Jimmie's skiff. The rescue made the front page of the "Anchorage Daily Times" and resulted in fame for the two friends. The newspaper called Frank and Wilbur "Alaska's very own moose wranglers."

As usual, on a November Saturday morning, Frank and Wilbur arose before anybody else and were down on the flats

with a string of decoys before first light. Hot coffee and anticipation, mixed with a bit of an attempt to stay warm, the boys
passed the morning till dawn to find a change in the weather.
The day before it had been a perfect goose day with gale-force
wind and driving horizontal rain. They brought down four of
the big honkers and several mallards before the school bell. But
on this day, as it got lighter, a sea fog developed, obscuring a
perfectly clear and sunny morning.

"Should of gone deer hunting over on the big island,"
Frank grunted.

"Yep," Wilbur replied. "I suppose if we had of, it would've
rained cats and dogs and blown us around till we were shivering
silly."

Frank removed his binoculars from the case to see if he
could x-ray through the low fog. "Damn, it's so calm out there,
the geese are probably asleep a half-a-mile offshore. Need somebody to run by in their boat to stir things up a bit. *Down!*"

Three green-winged teal came out of nowhere, almost
crashing into the top of Wilbur's famous duck blind. Frank
touched off one quick shot. One bird dropped in a half a dozen
pieces just a few feet behind them. "Nice blast, Frank. Maybe
we can each take home a piece."

"Damned kamikazes," Frank said. "Could've done less
damage by tripping them with my barrel."

"Yep, guess we could get a little shooting with this fog after all," Wilbur commented. "I think I'll take a look around, see
if the high tide brought in any sitters." He got up and shook
both legs to try to get the circulation back and limped off to the
west.

The fog broke overhead with an occasional patch of bright
blue. The tide was high. Wilbur had to slosh through a foot of
water towards the shore to get on dry land. When they had arrived in the dark, the shore was dry all the way to the blind. Ordinarily, the shooting was best just before high tide since the ris-

ing water stirred up the offshore ducks and brought them inland. The wind was calm, a sign of poor hunting. Frank sat tight thinking Wilbur might scare a bird his way. He thought about Cindy and his comfortable existence with her in this outdoor paradise. The night before they had talked about making their partnership official. The thought of marriage was not a clear one for either of them. They had both recoiled from previous relationships in pain. But this one was oddly comfortable. It was such a fluke—meeting her in the middle of a halibut opening up in the Bay. He chuckled out loud.

Boom! Frank ducked when he heard the shot. *Honk, Honk, Honk. Boom!*

Wilbur must have jumped a few geese in the fog. They were flying away. "Lucky son-of-a-bee." Frank muttered.

Wilbur stooped to grab the flopping honker. It was a big one, maybe twelve pounds. His second shot had missed—out of range. He twirled the big bird by the neck while keeping an eye out for more kamikazes. Something red floated ahead on the edge of the tide.

"Strange," Wilbur said out loud. A full plastic jug of gasoline bounced on the tide and sand. He bent down to pick up the jug and slung the goose onto his back. He went straight for the blind to show off his kill and the odd floating gas jug. The fog lifted as if a dimmer switch was turned up by nature's fog control panel. Any chance of more shooting had become remote.

"Going to be one nice day," Wilbur said as he snuck up behind Frank. Wilbur was beaming.

"Nice for you, you lucky jerk," Frank replied. "Did you shoot the gas jug too?"

"You bet! Brought it down from about a half-mile up. Darn thing was flying at the point of a perfect V-formation on its way south for the winter. By golly, there must've been a zillion of them." Wilbur's face was deadpan serious. He let a good pause linger. "It was just drifting along the beach, Frank."

"Just like you to score five gallons of gas," Frank retorted. The next thing you'll drag in will be the winning lottery ticket...full of four-shot."

They both stood silent by the blind. Frank envied the honker while Wilbur looked out toward the water, pretending to ignore Frank's jealous perusal of the big bird. Fog dispersed and moved upwards as they watched. Frank decided to sit again. Wilbur joined him and poured two cups of coffee. Geese honked, mallard ducks quacked in the distance. A bald eagle swooped down over them to chase a scooter off the water.

Something yellow floated in the tide a few yards ahead of the blind. Frank pushed himself up and walked out. "I'll be damned." He turned to show Wilbur a coil of good rope.

Wilbur looked hard again at the red gasoline jug. He grabbed the binoculars from Frank's hunting bag and scanned the beach with more scrutiny.

Frank found another coil of rope and brought it back to the blind.

"Looks like one of those Igloo coolers floating over there," Wilbur reported, binoculars in a perfect sniper's scan. "There's something green floating by it." He stood this time and made his way forthrightly out to the cooler.

Frank watched as Wilbur leaned to pick up the green object he had seen. He saw two ducks wind their way toward Wilbur. "Get down!" Frank yelled in a whisper, diving to the blind. The ducks veered off.

Wilbur stood out by his find and scanned the water out from the beach. He turned to Frank and yelled in full voice, "Frank, I think there's a problem here." He turned back to the water and said, "There's a lot of stuff washing up out here."

Frank walked out to where Wilbur stood. Wilbur handed Frank a wet green baseball hat and turned away. Another floating object caught his attention. He didn't say anything. A noisy flight of mallards flew right over them. Neither Frank nor

Wilbur noticed until it was too late.

Frank held the green hat and gawked as though confounded by it. A square patch above the cap's bill read, "Pelican Cold Storage."

"Shoot! I know this guy," Frank exclaimed. He swiftly stepped to the cooler. On top was a faded name of a boat. Sand and mud obscured the letters. He wiped it with his sleeve and his mouth dropped open. "'F/V Goblin'—damn." Roger never took that hat off when he was fishing, not even to take a nap. The sweat stain around the rim confirmed it. "Hey, Wilbur, get over here."

Wilbur returned with as much gear as he could carry. "What do you think?" he asked.

"I think we better get our butts home and call the Coast Guard," Frank replied with no hesitation. "It's Roger and that kid from Elfin Cove that broke his arm last year." Frank was hyperventilating.

"Let's go," Wilbur agreed and left on a run. The hunters left everything behind except for their guns and the goose.

"Yeah, this is Wilbur Cook from Humpback. I think we've found some debris from a boat accident. We tried reaching the vessel, 'F/V Goblin,' a crabber from Elfin Cove, on the radio with no luck." Wilbur fidgeted with his pocket knife as he talked into the radio. Frank and Cindy stood by him at the wheel of Tad Neff's fishing boat. By now, there was a gathering of people outside on the dock.

"Yeah, we found several pieces of boat gear, including a cooler of fresh food on the north side of Humpback Island. Yes, the side facing Gustavus," Wilbur reported. He answered many more of the Coast Guard's questions.

Someone ran to raise the local air charter service in Gustavus while Wilbur was busy on the phone. Within minutes the pilot was in the air. Cruising out from the Island Tails where Wilbur and Frank found the debris, it didn't take long to spot the boat capsized in about twenty-five feet of water not a hundred yards offshore. From the air, the pilot saw no sign of survivors.

The entire island searched for two days for Roger and his crew. Jimmie notified Roger's wife by marine radio from his boat. Searching for his friends from his fishing boat around the clock, Jimmie refused to give up hope that somehow they had made it to shore.

About noon on the second day, a Coast Guard diver found Roger on the bottom, just a few yards from the boat. Hearts sunk in a universal wave of disappointment and grief.

The search continued for two more days for Roger's young crew, but not until the following spring did the mystery resolve. A couple of hikers found the young man's swollen body ashore, again only a few yards from where the "Goblin" had suddenly sunk the fall before.

For a time Frank and Wilbur wondered if they'd ever go hunting again. The "Goblin" disaster had kind of taken the serenity out of a good, old-fashioned duck hunt. Life is tough at times on Southeast Alaska's coast. Fishing is dangerous, as is flying, hunting, kayaking, and just plain living. Everybody has a friend or family member who left for a day or two on an ordinary excursion, never to return to tell about it.

Frank and Wilbur took a few weekends off from their duck blinds to be with their families and reflect on their fragile place on this earth. But with the first heavy snowfall, they loaded up the skiff and went across Icy Strait to Point Adolphus for their annual deer hunt. On the way back Frank's skiff took on water in a gale. Breaking seas pummeled over the bow. Quick and lucky maneuvers by the two old friends got them home with two wet deer and a case of the jitters.

"Guess when I have to pack it in, I'd just as soon do it here," Wilbur said over a brandy at Frank's kitchen table.

"Yeah, but please don't pull the plug yet," Frank admonished. "Anyway, here's to Roger," Frank said as he hoisted his mug. "At least he didn't get run over by an L.A. drunk."

Wilbur continued to build his hunting blinds. However, of late, the master duck hunter has confessed to lots of hunts and not even a few ducks. "The older I get," he said, "the harder it is to shoot something. Life is too damned short. I'm beginning to wonder how short it is for all of God's critters." Wilbur scratched his mustache and pulled his ear to continue, "But, on the other hand, to hook a big fish, now that's a whole different story."

Wilbur kept with him a reminder of that fateful duck hunt. He mounted that big Canada goose. Darlene stuffed it for him later that winter. Around the goose's neck he hung a brass plaque which read, "The Goblin." On the honker's head, he had Darlene sew the green baseball cap with the sweat ring. When people asked him what the hat was all about, Wilbur's face would turn a little gray and then he would say, "Just a little reminder of one weird duck hunt on Humpback Island. You know, life can be pretty damned short."

In the fall, Wilbur and Frank continued to get together for an annual hunt or two. Rarely did a day on the flats go by without one of them saying something like, "Remember that damned duck hunt?" A shared silent look out across the waters of Glacier Bay to the Fairweather Mountains and the long stretch of low beach where it all happened brought back the memory of why they were here, why they risked it. They had both accepted the chance of not making it home to tell another story. One of them would always break the silence and say, "Well, better out here than on some damned bozo-land freeway down south."

"Ditto," Wilbur would reply. "Hey...duck, ya ol' jerk." Two mallards squawked overhead. "Let me show you how to..."

Frank got the jump on his friend. "Boom, Boom, Boom..."

Chapter 13

Contagion

WINTER IS THE TIME OF YEAR WHEN HUMPBACK Islanders prepare for the onslaught of those nasty little critters that fly between us, around us, and inside us to cause all sorts of ugly aches, pains, coughs, and sneezes. We swear that something about our Southeast Alaska climate creates a neon sign in the sky above the Panhandle that reads, "VACANCY—NASTY FLU VIRUSES—ALL TYPES WELCOME HERE"

Then when the rain gets beating to a rhythm predisposing a harmony with a massive snowfall, and the ice builds mountainous two-rut sculptures on our roads, we all go inside and lock ourselves in with the ugly little creatures that make us miserable and wish for spring. At the height of all the closeness, the radio reports that the State Health Department tells us what we already know. Some critter from Hong Kong, Puerto Rico, Fairbanks or Denver spotted our neon sign and now is comfortably dispersing contagion and misery.

But when the winter sets in and the nights get long and cold, other contagious things have happened. The hunkered-down human closeness that spreads germs can also breed a different kind of epidemic. The few hardy wintering islanders got to know each other very well, to say the least. More importantly, they had a considerable influence on one another.

A few flu seasons ago, our tiny island community experienced an event similar to one of the terrible virus epidemics, although there were no little bacterial meanies to blame. It was a cryptic combination of close friends and neighbors, rain, snow, ice, and bitter cold that caused this outbreak. And, no doubt, it was not the only known occurrence of this sort of social epidemic.

On any given winter day there was a reason to get together with one or more of the neighbors, virus outbreaks or not. Sometimes it all started from a shared cup of coffee, or somebody needed to borrow a special tool for a critical project. Several necessary chores took the hand of a neighbor, such as raising an interior wall for a new bedroom or repairing a boat engine. Once the first contact was made, it was not unusual to have the whole day become an impromptu social event.

One January day, Sara went to Cindy's to borrow an "L.L. Bean" catalog. Gus had dropped by to catch his usual noon-time "The Price Is Right" on television. Soon after, Delia dropped over to say hello. Then Darlene showed up looking for a stepladder. Cindy's husband Frank and Sara's husband Jimmie were busy pulling out Frank's pickup engine, and Darlene gave them a hand and forgot to get her ladder.

Aunt Bess saw all the commotion when she took her daily stroll over to the post office. Over morning coffee, she and Beth had just removed a batch of fresh bread from the oven. Beth fetched two loaves from Aunt Bess's house and joined in. Cindy couldn't resist the temptation to pull out some homemade coffee liqueur, and the party went full bore till late afternoon.

The big news for the day at this extemporaneous get-together was that Wilbur's wife, Laura, was pregnant. This particular source of excitement for the little collection of folks had considerable consequence. Laura and Wilbur had been more or less free spirited and independent in their lifestyle. While they both were genuinely wonderful with everybody else's kids, they had always said, "Kids? Oh…maybe someday, but not right now. We have too much we want to do; you know, travel and stuff."

In the nighttime darkness of a first Alaskan cold-snap, Wilbur and Laura held each other tight after a hearty dinner and a rare bottle of cheap wine. Little did they realize at the time that usual precautions had been neglected. When strange things started happening to Laura's body over Christmas, it necessitated an unexpected trip to Juneau. She called her friend, Cindy, with the news. Frank had to call Gus for some oxygen for poor Cindy. Her screams were so clamorous, Frank ran in from the woodpile, grabbed the first-aid kit from the entryway and expected to find burns or blood at the scene of the noise. Instead, he found his wife apparently physically unharmed, but gasping in laughter and tears, sprawled against the kitchen counter. Gus walked in with an antique bottle of oxygen, and he and Frank checked vital signs. "It's only female hysteria," Gus claimed. "My wife had it three or four times a year. Give her a little space and she'll shake out of it soon enough."

Cindy, a devout believer in childlessness, and Laura were the closest of friends. It was one of those kind of friendships that helped a person make it through a hard winter and occasional tiffs with one's mate. Frank and Wilbur's friendship promoted Laura and Cindy's. When the boys went off hunting, the women would plan a day at the beach gathering garden seaweed. The couples often went fishing together or took trips to Juneau or Sitka together. Wilbur and Laura stood up for their good friends at the amazing event of their Juneau courthouse marriage. Most importantly, the two couples remained childless together.

When Cindy broke the news to her neighbors, Aunt Bess had the first response, "Oh, my lord!" she exclaimed. "Is their life going to change or what?"

Sara was elated. Her youngest was just two at the time. When Cindy and Laura took spur-of-the-moment trips to the city, Sara had to stay behind with her children. She mumbled half under her breath, "It's about time those two got serious and settled down."

Later that night, Cindy and Frank were cleaning up from

the day's events when Cindy said to Frank, "Laura claimed it was an accident. Huh. But now that she's really, uh, you know...pregnant, God, they're tickled silly over the idea."

"Yeah, that Wilbur wasn't worth a tinker's damn last week," Frank added. "He'll probably be absolutely worthless waste come spring king fishing season."

"I don't know. Guess I always thought I'd have a baby some day," Cindy reflected. "Some day always seems like tomorrow, not today."

"I was telling Jimmie that if I had a kid now, I'd be fifty-five years old when he graduated from high school," Frank said. "Guess I'm not getting any younger. Next year I'd be fifty-six."

"Here I am almost thirty years old!" Cindy agreed. "Criminy, I suffer from the delusion that I'm still in high school!"

"You look a heck of a lot better than any seventeen-year-old-teeny-bopper I know," Frank replied.

"And you're a sweet blind fool," Cindy cried. She made a sexy gesture with her hips and blushed crimson. One compliment led to another and the epidemic had begun. Cindy and Frank made passionate love that night. So did Jimmie and Sara after a similar discussion.

A week or so later, Darlene netted a winter romance, a rugged looking carpenter from Juneau who disappeared come spring. Laura's celebrated condition, however, made her recall the sentimental notion of childbirth with abandon. She had always wanted her daughter to have a brother, husband or not.

From one cabin to the next, from one impromptu social gathering to another, the emotional virus multiplied and spread throughout the tiny community. Beginning in June that year, there were seven new babies by Halloween. Six years later, the school enrollment grew to needing two full-time teachers; one teacher for the first graders and one for all the other kids.

Among other things, conception can be every bit as contagious as any other darn bug on Humpback Island.

Chapter 14

Human Changes

EVERYBODY ON HUMPBACK ISLAND AND THE mainland in Gustavus expressed their surprise when Bert Johnson, an old-time Gustavusite, sold off most of his homestead in Gustavus and moved all of his equipment to a nice place on the top of the Island. Some thought he was plumb crazy; others admired his sense of adventure. His chosen ground bordered the road that he had pioneered when he Jack, Hank, and Dan had first arrived there by accident. He told most people that he was bored with the politics and new growth over in Gustavus and just plain wanted some new dirt to move around and a change of view from the old one on his back porch. According to Dan and Gus, this was Bert's answer to a new place to take a pee. In other words, a urinary-grounds solution to a mid-life crisis—a change of pasture.

But with the issue of ownership of the island heating up to a pending court ruling, Hank, Dan, and Jack urged Bert to make the move. He was the only bachelor among the group, had plenty of money and land, and assured everybody that a chance at new scenery was fine with him. Not only that, he was one of those rare nice guys that nobody could argue with or dislike. They figured if Bert went and made the move, he would be the original island land-claimer's best ambassador. If they had any claim to ownership of the island, the current residents would have a hard time being nasty to him, regardless of some differences of opinion about island ownership.

When Bert, his son, and Ol' Gus pulled two homemade

barges full of equipment, including a dump truck, a backhoe and a grader, not to mention volumes of home and shop building supplies, plus a load of hardware and tools on Captain Gitgo's landing craft, the community of Humpback's humble natives were speechlessly amazed. Frank and Cindy's benefactor Dan came along for the work party and so did Jack and his entire brood of children.

Within a week, the crew had a nice road punched in up over the top of the island, a 1,500 square foot home framed and camped in because it was raining, and a 3,000 square foot roofed shed to keep all the equipment and tools dry. Gus, Frank, Tad, Jimmie, and even Weird John showed up to help each day. The result was a fifteen-odd work crew that seemed to have more fun than not. Many times the jokes poked outnumbered the nails pounded. Bert was such a generous guy. He flew in fresh food and a few cases of cold beer and pop each day. By the end of the week, Humpback Island had now acquired its uppermost encampment, not to mention its most well-built structures and finest equipment.

Most of the local help conked out after one weekend to the next. Besides, Dan, Gus, and Bert had the project well under control. But then there were the women. Bert, who had a repu- tation of staying away from mixed gatherings in Gustavus and being rather shy when it came to the advances of available fe- males, found himself inundated by the industrious and caring ladies of Humpback when it came time to make his new house "homey," or, in other words, fit for a woman's presence. Aunt Bess made curtains from a variety of old towels, sheets, and unused dresses. Cindy insisted, "you can't have a bathroom without stained molding, a carpet by the shower, and a towel rack, not to mention a toilet tissue rack." Bert didn't have the guts to argue. Beth put the kitchen in order, complete with fresh bread, homemade blueberry pie and chocolate-chip cookies.

By the end of three weeks, Bert's new Humpback home

was a castle. It sat atop the second highest peak with views to most sides. As an afterthought, Dan added a crow's nest—a third floor for the purpose of gaining the perfect view of Glacier Bay, Point Adolphus, and the hump on Pleasant Island. Dan said, "You can sit up here and watch the boats in trouble and the tourists harass the whales. When the fish come in, your marine radio will be very busy, I'm sure."

Gus added, "Heck, a guy could spot deer on three islands, a bull moose on the mainland side, and me coming and going from my outhouse."

With all the community support, Bert felt a little guilty about his first reason for moving over—to stake his claim on the land, that is. With time, he dismissed his original reason, without telling Hank and Jack. Dan was a little more community-minded about the ownership business. Dan explained, "You have to admire their wanting to have one place in Southeast where the loggers, subdividers, developers, federal control junkies, and the miners don't run over the people or take over the land."

Gus answered with a resounding, "Yeah, by golly. You have a point there. I moved over for the same darned reason."

And Bert just shook his head up and down and said, "Uh-huh."

"Now Bert, a pleasant looking man in his mid-forties was considered by many to be a real, but very hard-to-get catch in the romance/partner arena. He had means, property, manners, cleanliness, and that always adorable shyness. Nonetheless, Bert seemed to pay no attention, other than to be polite, to just about any female he ran across. He was famous for always saying, "Thank you, ma'am; I beg your pardon, ma'am. Is there anything I could help you with, ma'am?" Any he did help most every woman, married or not, in some way or another. Aunt Bess's toilet overflowed—Bert was there. Beth had a stack fire while Tad was out fishing—Bert was there.

However, the standard rumor heard most often was that when Bert's wife and kids ran off on him when he was working up on the oil pipeline, it plumb broke his heart real darn good. After that he became more and more shy, extremely polite, and definitely not in the market for romance, at least not looking in from the outside. Inside, he was lonely as hell. The more humanly sensitive and understanding residents on Humpback knew this full well, especially the old-timers like Aunt Bess and Ol' Gus.

Well, as it usually goes, some of the people on Humpback had one of those impromptu get-together sort of eat-and-gossip meetings over at Wilbur and Laura's one day. The vote, although she was obviously absent, was for Darlene to make a secret attempt but by now a very well known neighborly play for the "Bert-the-man Merchandise." He was only ten years her senior and they had a lot in common—like being able to make or fix anything.

But the darndest thing happened after the match started up. Darlene had her rather well-fixed opinions on how a seal should go on an oil pan gasket, and Bert did too. Of course, Bert's opinion, while apparently not the same as Darlene's, was very much different than the two of them could happily agree upon. Darlene stomped off in a huff swearing Bert had his head up somewhere it shouldn't be. So much for that match-up.

Then something happened that was certainly unpredicted by the most astutely minded in town. Bert started to drop by Tad and Beth's for coffee and a piece of that great pie. Then it turned out that Bert played the guitar and Beth had picked up the mandolin somewhere along the way. Beth then started blessing Bert with excursions on her three-wheeler to deliver various baked goods and play a lick or two. They became great and regular friends. Tad didn't have a clue—he was fishing most of the time. "Good season," he told Beth when she complained of his more-than-usual fishing excursions.

Then, for heaven's sake, something magical happened on one of Beth's trips up to Bert's. She kissed him on the cheek and gave him a rather longish hug and said, "Thank you." Beth turned to leave and Bert just stood there completely hypnotized. Beth was long gone when Bert found himself still standing at his doorway—must have been hours.

By and by, the fishing season came to a close and Tad noticed a real difference in the household. It took him awhile because when fishing ends, hunting starts. Beth seemed to be gone an awful lot compared to before—before the fishing season. Then, Tad noticed that in years past, Beth had usually waited for him after a hunt to help clean up. Many times now, Beth came after dark, hours after the mess.

"Where have you been?" Tad would ask.

And Beth would answer, "Oh, you know, out visiting. Sorry I'm so late."

Well, as the story goes, Tad went out on an overnight deer hunt with his friends Frank and Wilbur.

Beth chose this night to not come home. And Bert, while nervous as a first-grader in his first school play, did not disagree.

Of course, little gets by the locals. Aunt Bess saw Beth head up to Bert's that evening and not return till about ten the next morning. Aunt Bess told Cindy and Cindy told Frank when he got back with his limit of deer. As it usually goes, the word was scattered all around within a day or two with one exception—it hadn't gotten to Tad.

Then one Saturday night the men decided on a penny-ante poker party. Beth knew these usually went late. So she went up to Bert's, who didn't gamble. No doubt the rest of the story can be guessed. Beth and Bert got carried away and Beth just said, "Oh, what the heck, the whole town knows anyway. I guess it's Tad's turn. I owe that to him—he's our friend." Bert, being the nice guy he was, gulped and started to sweat a little. "Are you sure?" he asked.

"I think I am," Beth replied. "Oh, darn, Bert, I know I am." Their embrace lasted throughout the night. When Tad first returned home about two a.m. that night, he quietly removed his day clothes, donned his night sweats, climbed into his side of bed, and fell into one of those immediate beer-laden slumbers. It was not till about five in the morning when his bladder woke him up that he noticed Beth was not next to him.

A slight hangover and all, he climbed down the stairs to check the couch. Empty. Two aspirin and a cup of instant coffee and he began to worry. Within an hour, he called Frank and Cindy. Cindy talked Frank into going over to Tad's and trying to break the news. When Frank arrived at Tad's, the outside morning was breaking with a dark overcast—so was the inside morning. Tad was at the table still drinking coffee and shaking like a leaf. Rarely did he smoke, but Tad had a folder of "Drum" for those special occasions. As far as Frank cold tell, he'd smoked several.

Frank made some real coffee without saying more than "Howdy, Tad," then sat down across from him. "What's up, buddy?" Frank asked.

Tad squirmed and ashed his cigarette in his coffee without noticing. "No Beth," he replied. "Something's up—has been for a while."

There was a long silence except for the slurping and puffing. Frank finally broke it. "Tad, buddy, it happens to the best of us. At least it happened to me once."

"What in the hell happens to the best of us?" Tad shouted.

"You know, women get to thinking different now and again," Frank started. "Tad...Tad, I hate to be the one to tell you this, but Beth is kind of mixed up with old Bert up on the hill."

Tad lit another sloppily rolled cigarette. Frank reached for the bag of "Drum" to roll his own. Silence.

"You know what, Frank?" Tad finally said out of the blue: "I feel like a pile of dog doo-doo that's been stepped on and wiped on the edge of a curb."

All Frank could say was, "Yes, yes, I've felt that way before."

The meeting went on for some hours. Wilbur came over and helped Frank put Tad into a sort of male coma.

Beth showed up later when Frank, Tad, and Wilbur were in the middle of a slam-dunk-the-female-species discussion. She packed some clothes and things, came down the stairs and said, "I'm sorry, Tad. I loved you. It just happened. But I can't be a fisherman's wife anymore. Really, I'm sorry."

And the change was made that day, consummated by a divorce in the springtime, and a Bert-and-Beth party and common-law ceremony on the summer solstice. Tad even came to the party. He brought Darlene. Or maybe it was Darlene who brought Tad.

Chapter 15

Weird John's E.P.A.

WHEN IT COMES TO THE END OF THE LIFE OF AN outhouse hole, one most typically procrastinates the digging of a new respite site as long as possible—meaning just prior to overflow. However, in this case, the neighbors complained; Aunt Bess especially. One day she finally got up the nerve to wander over to Weird John's and say, "For heaven's sake, John, you're stinking up the whole island. I can't smell my prize petunias nor my lupine, only your darned outhouse. Every time I bake a pie, it smells less of fresh berries and more of fresh you." Bess handed John a shovel and stomped back down the path.

Now, as most folks know, there are several little tricks to keeping an outhouse fresh. One is by scattering layers of sawdust in the hole on a regular basis. Another is by carefully burning the hole with refuse oil or diesel fuel. In an effort to postpone the move of his outhouse and the rigorous effort of the dig, Weird John tried both at once.

It had been an unusually dry week or two. John had been cutting firewood and had a nice pile of fresh, dry sawdust. He also had a stash of number one kerosene fuel for lighting his oil lamps. The shovel was put to use hauling sawdust—a lot of sawdust. He then doused his pile of sawdust with a gallon or two of kerosene and John thought he had effectively procrastinated the new hole digging/outhouse moving routine. He thought he had better things to do.

As it went, however, Weird John torched off the island's first complete cleansing of an outhouse. It burned to the ground within fifteen minutes. "Damn," John said later, "that was at least five dollars worth of kerosene."

The following day, now outhouse-less, John covered his ashen first outhouse with fresh sand and then set about the two projects of digging a new hole and building a new shelter for his morning constitution. He decided to build a shelter first and use little holes scattered about for the time being since on his first effort to dig a new hole he hit something extremely hard about one foot beneath the surface. He moved a foot or two and tried again with the same bad luck. A few hours into the building project, he decided to cut a few young alder trees dangerously close to his existing tent site. He'd recently been thinking of moving his tent anyway in order to get higher, dryer ground and get a bit further away, of course from his own refuse.

After cleaning his belongings out from the tent, he noticed that the tent floor had acquired large holes as if acid had been poured on it. He moved the tent after cutting the bottom out, timbered the young alder around the old tent site for roof joists and studs for his new outhouse, laid a new tarp floor for the upper portion of his remaining pieces of tent several yards from the original site and called it a day.

The next morning, John tried to dig a small hole for his morning meditation and again hit something quite hard yards away from the test holes he had tried the day before. Regardless, he moved a nice beach log to the site of the shallow hole and read his favorite magazine, "Soldier of Fortune." Once finished, he covered the little hole, made a nice breakfast of oatmeal and salmon bits, and went back to work on his new alder-framed outhouse. In one day, he had a nice little structure covered with a camouflage tarp and a chainsaw-milled, beach log door. Again he called it a day.

The next day, he repeated the digging routine from the morning before and started a hole only to hit something hard about eight inches beneath the surface sand. Now he was curious. After all, for three days he'd tried to dig an outhouse hole in locations spread over an acre or so and was thwarted rudely by something extremely hard not far below the surface. He grabbed his shovel in frustration this time and was determined to find an answer no matter that his clock-like inner needs were calling loudly to his lower torso. Holding onto his morning physical needs with great grit, John scraped and dug until he had exposed a large battery—a very old black battery. Inscribed on the top was a small metal tag that read, "Property of the U.S. ARMY." The battery was large, and it took him another round of digging and the leverage of a shovel handle to finally lift it from the sludge and set it kind of cockeyed on a nearby rock. Something the color of a reddish-yellow ooze dripped from one twist-on cap. Now, John, being no city slicker, knew the smell and taste of sulfuric acid. What he had discovered was an acid-filled battery which appeared to be at least forty or more years old with a label claiming it was the property of the army.

A nice hole now deeply dug into the sand, John fetched his tissue and beach log and favorite magazine, sat down and contemplated his find. As soon as everything came out okay, he went back to one of his earlier hole attempts, dug and scraped feverishly, and found a slightly smaller battery of the same make. This time it was more like a foot deep, and again in a hole of what was once ocean bottom beach sand.

Now, Weird John had gotten to know his top-of-the island neighbors, Bert and Bess. John played the harmonica and became an occasional member of their covered porch jam sessions. John trusted Bert not to flap his mouth with good reason. Bert had known about and ignored John's small crop of marijuana and let him smoke his marijuana pipe on his porch during the height of music heaven.

"Army, huh," Bert said.

"Yeah. I bet there's a few hundred of them at least, scattered around my campsite. Heck right under my now acid-burned tent. The battery acid must have leaked and seeped up to the surface, burning the bottom out of my poor tent."

"Ya know, when the army had their airstrip and communications site over in Gustavus, they must have dumped all their old batteries overboard; sort of a marine dump. Hell, and they land underneath you. Ha, isn't that an odd one for ya'," Bert said."

Bess piped in from the kitchen, "I'll bet you a nickel that no army official ever expected an earthquake to expose their bad environmental habits."

Bess now came into the large living room. "Somebody should call the EPA or the U.S. Army Corps of Engineers or something. We can't have poor John sleeping on a bed of acid."

"Now, let's think about this," Bert said. "It would seem to me that with all these environmentalists running amuck around here, that the army dumping lethal materials forty or fifty years ago would mean a nickel for somebody now. Nobody wants poor John or any other critter sleeping on battery acid."

"No kidding," John replied. He started checking his arms for burns.

Weird John, Bess, and Bert kept this all a secret longer than could have been imaginable on Humpback. But when two strange official-looking men flew in from Gustavus a few weeks later and hired Bert's backhoe to conduct a test dig, the secret was out. A few scoops dug by Bert's backhoe where John's tent had been before he moved it, told the real story. The first scoop brought a mountain of old batteries and encrusted radio gear. A few more scoops dug from a variety of locations around John's encampment brought much more of the same, including spools of cooper wire eaten by the saltwater.

Understandable to some, I suppose, the U.S. Army had reason to keep this wanton trash dump somewhat quiet, and the U.S. Environmental Protection Agency, feeling rather gung-ho about a new project in beautiful, pristine Alaska hit rather head on with the army in a meeting in Washington.

The EPA wanted to go out to public bid and make a big scuttle over the matter. The army wanted to keep it as hushed-up as could ever be. In the end, the army won the battle under one condition, that the EPA be required to keep an oversight manager on the project at all times, and that the greatest precautions be taken not to hurt or harm anyone or anything else.

Bert, being a respected, bonded, and licensed contractor provided the best way to keep the little project as quiet as possible. And between Bert's equipment, Weird John's labor, and Ol' Gus's barge, the waste removal could be quietly executed with little fuss. The army, however, agreed to shore up the community dock under Bert's supervision and once the locals got wind of the whole affair, they agreed that a better dock and keeping things as quiet as possible would protect what little anonymity they had left.

In the end, even those against such a hullabaloo over a few old batteries kind of grew to like the idea. Every able-bodied person in town was hired to help at Davis-Bacon wages—Twenty something dollars per hour. Weird John got a sizeable sum for his incredible find from the EPA and the army had to pick up the whole tab. By and by, the dock is new and Weird John's original campsite is now the community park. Weird John built a permanent shelter with his windfall. The EPA site manager saw fit to haul in some landscaping material to make the mess look in its final stages like it had been the only older growth region on a new growth piece of land.

And, most of all, everybody in town took a winter vacation to a southern resort on their bonus earnings.

Weird John stays from October to April each year on the Baja peninsula where he has a flush toilet.

Chapter 16

Humpback Island N.U.U.U.T.S.

SOON AFTER CAPTAIN SAN DIEGO FINISHED HIS NEW lodge, a collection of save-the-wilderness organizations from London, San Francisco, Washington, D.C., Los Angeles, and Anchorage filed suit against the State of Alaska and several departments of the federal government. Their suit stated that all those named were guilty of dragging their feet on protecting a unique, untamed environment—Humpback Island.

On the surface of the concerns addressed to the court by the wilderness folks was the increasing number of humpback whales seen in the vicinity of the island. Second to that, the plaintiffs celebrated the geological miracle that shaped the island making it appear at a distance to be a whale. There was obvious speculation that the island actually attracted the whales with its whale-like shape.

Regardless of the island's incomparable flora and fauna, the truth of the matter, however, was that court action had already been initiated by a whole bunch of parties regarding the contested ownership of the piece of new land. Throughout most of Humpback's history, therefore, no ownership had been clearly defined. The island's fate was hopelessly tied up in various levels of the state's and nation's courts. *Nobody* owned Humpback Island. Most of the people who lived there preferred it that way. That is, all but one.

Sometime after Captain San Diego had spent a bunch of his money on a new frame lodge, he began to fear for the survival and perpetuation of his investment. When he made his original bet, it hadn't dawned on him that if he didn't own the land the lodge occupied, there might be an increasingly strong possibility that someone else might eventually gain title to it. Needless to say, the captain came around to having a little fear about the matter when he realized he had spent his entire retirement on the place. He had a problem.

Not being a stupid man, the captain hedged his bet by joining forces with Brad Stewart to search for and catch the wily sandfish, or tricka-tricka. Hence, he invested the lion's share, along with some of his Japanese friends, in the up-front money required to purchase the odd little processing ship to look for the tricka-tricka and hopefully become rich on the sale of the fish to the Japanese, regardless of the possible loss in the Weyindeheydya Lodge. However, months into the project, Brad had only come up with a few pounds. Brad was convinced that the only stockpile of the tricka-tricka was somewhere in the National Park. In fact, he was cited more than once by the whale patrol for nearly every possible infraction, including night boat traffic and fishing for an unknown fish without state or federal regulation, season, or oversight. Ranger Rick had even cited Brad for indecent exposure while swimming naked with three female crew members—a Princess Lines Cruise ship had somehow come rather close to them without their notice. Whoops. The ship's Park Service Naturalist radioed in to headquarters, "Four naked humans are seen off the port bow." She had forgotten to turn off her ship hailer and the entire tourist population got a good peek.

But the current list of contested owners of Humpback Island included everybody from the U.S. Government and the State of Alaska to one Native group and a half dozen people from Gustavus. According to court records then, everybody in the country had at least one piece of the action. If you were a Tlingit Indian from Hoonah and both an Alaskan and a U.S. citizen, you had three more chances to get title to the Wayindaheydya Conifer Lodge's land than Captain San Diego. The key to the captain's fear was hidden in the word "country." Captain San Diego was not a U.S. citizen; he was Japanese with a green card.

In the prime of the tourist season, Captain San Diego celebrated the grand opening of the new lodge by sending out invitations and notices to just about everybody he could think of. He invited all of his old cruise ship buddies and the good people of Humpback Island. He notified the newspapers, the travel agencies and the National Park Service in hopes of drumming up a solid business.

One of the first guests to the week-long opening was an international environmentalist from New York named Clifford Leslie Pierpont III. Clifford, or Cliffy to his close friends, brought with him a ladyfriend from London who carried six cases of camera gear, another girlfriend from Washington, D.C. who reportedly had a direct line to the editor of the "Post," and a twenty-four-year-old friend and movie stuntman from L.A. who liked to fish. Cindy met them at the Gustavus airport.

Climbing from the small sleek jet, Cliffy handed Cindy one of his carry-ons and then turned to help his girlfriend, Penny. They were the perfect picture of an advertisement for L.L. Bean. Nikon and Sony cameras hung from each shoulder. Bushnell and Gerber adorned their belts. Penny looked like she had come from a page of Nordstrom's Christmas catalog.

Gary, the stuntman, wore a dirty California T-shirt, torn Levi 501s, a handmade New Zealand lamb's wool sweater tied loosely around his neck, and Birkenstock sandals. Jessica, the freelance photographer from London, dressed in various undressed stages of arctic winter gear. The deep vee of her sweater certainly wouldn't keep much, if anything, warm.

"Hi," said Cindy to all of them at once. "Guess I'm the Humpback Island greeter. I'll give you a ride to our boat."

"Seen any whales?" Cliffy asked.

"All the time," Cindy replied.

Cindy led them into a worn-out Chevy van with a picture of a befuddled whale and the name of the lodge on the side. Pieces of the van's floorboards were missing. Road dust coated everything. She slid open the side door and said, "Welcome to the limo. Jump on in."

Jessica began to climb into the side door, stopped abruptly and wiped the second seat with her index finger. She was rudely obvious about it. "I can't put my gear in here!" Jessica exclaimed.

"You can walk," Cindy replied nonchalantly. "It's only about ten miles. Dressed like that, maybe one of the local boys will show you around. I can run the boat back for you tomorrow."

Jessica looked at Penny, then back at the van. "Got any plastic bags?" she asked.

"For what?" Cindy replied, having become a little irate with this uppity bunch.

"Just get your ass the hell in, Jessica," Cliffy said. "It's been in dirtier places than that van. Plus you have your pants on." He grabbed her bags of cameras, covered them with his rain parka, and put them up on the seat. "If we wanted no dirt, we would have gone to Disneyland."

Jessica turned to Cliffy and gave him one of her flirtingly-most-devilish looks, then punched him in the shoulder.

On the ride to the National Park dock in Bartlett Cove, Gary fell asleep astraddle the luggage in the rear seat. Jessica fussed about the dust the entire trip. She used a designer scarf to wipe her cleavage. Penny oohed and awed the whole bumpy time about how green everything was. Cliffy wanted to know if the lodge had a fax machine.

"Sorry, no fax machine," Cindy said. "But we do have a single pay telephone on the front porch of the Park lodge."

Cliffy turned white and looked as if he could go into shock.

"Uh...uh...how far is this Humpback Island from the Park head-quarters?" he asked.

"Plus or minus fifteen miles by boat or plane," Cindy said. "We have a good marine radio."

"Oh, my God! Can we stop a minute at the Park?" Cliffy asked. "Guess I need to use the phone."

"Golly, Cliffy honey, if we wanted to have instant access to the office, we would have gone to Central Park," Jessica teased.

After they turned down the ramp road to the dock, Cindy parked and pointed to the visitor's information office. "You can get a phone upstairs outside the restaurant, a map, a bathroom, and a lecture in there. Bring your gear to the boat when you come. The boat leaves for Humpback in thirty minutes."

Cindy carried an armload of gear to the boat. As planned, she called the lodge with her marine radio. Sara, the cook, answered the call.

"Are you ready over there, Sara?" Cindy asked. "We have some real...ah...wilderness fanatics coming." Cindy chuckled.

"Yeah. I hope they like fish; I hear they could be vegetarian," Sara replied.

"I don't know, but they're a pain in the neck otherwise. I figure they'll be the type that talk a good line about protecting the wilderness but can't stand to be near it," Cindy said. "Already had a real scene about a fax machine."

"They will like our rooms with a shared bath down the hall, won't they?" Sara said while laughing.

"I'll tell the ladies we only have a two-holer out back. *Ha!*" Cindy said. "We'll see you in a little while, if I don't lose them overboard."

The foursome received quite an education in the Park visitor's office. Ranger Rick, now the Chief Ranger, informed them that "Humpback Island is occupied by renegade outlaws and squatters."

"You shouldn't stay over there with that bunch," Rick said.

"They will all be thrown off Humpback when the courts get around to it."

"Why is that?" Cliffy asked.

"Well, they just squatted on it with nobody's official permission. I think they're trying to steal it from the National Park," Rick replied. "The day after the island came up in an earthquake, I had to arrest a couple of developers over there for fighting over it. The very same day, the superintendent notified Washington and applied for protective wilderness status. Not a few days later, a couple of hippies showed up and squatted on it. Now there's a Japanese-owned tourist trap. I suppose that's where you're staying, aren't you?" Rick asked.

"Yes, it is," Penny replied forthrightly. "And that 'Japanese-owned' lodge, or rather our host, invited us personally as his guests. He's a friend of Cliffy's." Penny's comments proved successful. The ranger became momentarily speechless, an unusual condition for him.

Cliffy had been using the telephone in the inner office. He emerged from his conversation with New York and asked Penny, "What's all the chatter about? Is something wrong with our plans?"

"Sure as hell is!" A tall and graying mid-sixties-age man dressed in brown coveralls and a fishing vest entered the small visitor's office. He glared at the ranger, not saying anything. Everyone turned at once to take a look at him.

Finally, a young woman with a brass nameplate that said "Naturalist" said, "Hi there, Hank. What can we do for you? Going fishing?"

"Yes, I sure am," Hank said. I just wondered if you guys are allowing fishing up Glacier Bay anymore. Heard you were protecting it from everything and everybody, even at night. Guess you have to be a parkie or a biologist to go up there anymore. Confounded government gestapo these days. I pay my taxes, too. You'd think this was a private club, not a taxpayer-owned national park."

"Slow down, Hank," Ranger Rick said. "You can go sport fishing in some areas if you have a vessel permit. Just don't break the speed limit in the whale waters, and here's a map. The pink areas are closed to motor vessels. The purple areas are closed to nighttime boat traffic one-half hour after the official sunset until one-half hour before the sunrise. The gray areas are closed beaches due to bear sightings. Stay a good mile away from all the islands, they're closed for bird nesting. Otherwise, fishing is allowed, with a vessel permit that is."

"You didn't leave much fishing ground, Ranger," Hank remarked. "I might as well fish over by Humpback or Adolphus where I can get near the coastline."

Gary's ears perked up when he heard about the fishing. "How's the fishing by Humpback Island?" he asked.

"Okay for now," Hank replied. "You better hurry up, though. The Japanese are there fishing the hell out of it, the Park wants to close it, and the Natives want to keep it in sacred trust. As soon as the court pulls their lazy government butts out of the easy chair, I'll own most of it."

"Don't believe a word from Ol' Hank here," Rick interrupted. "He wants to subdivide the whole island. If he were to win the court battle, he would own it lock, stock, and barrel until he sold it for the highest dollar."

"I was the first one there," Hank said, pointing his finger at Rick. "If the Park had it, nobody would get to use it except prissies with the right kind of college degree."

The naturalist couldn't resist adding her two cents to the argument. Meek and very polite, she carefully said, "Well, I think the State ought to get Humpback Island. They want to turn it into a preserve. And a preserve wouldn't prevent some human use."

"I like that idea, too," Jessica said. It sounds to me like a state preserve would cause the least harm and allow the most people to enjoy it. You know, our wilderness association filed an injunction with the court to allow us to be a party to this unfortunate dilemma." Jessica's British accent was obvious.

"Another foreigner trying to run our business," Hank replied. "Now we have the local Natives, the Japanese, the British, the Feds, the State and the Greenies—where's all this nonsense going to end? I just want to go fishing in what used to be a nice place to wet a line!" Hank turned and stomped off.

"Sure, fish on his own private Island," Rick remarked after Hank walked outside.

Cindy, still at the boat, began to wonder what the hold-up was all about. She told the guests just thirty damned minutes. She checked her watch for the fourth time, climbed up the ramp and made her way back to the visitor's office in hopes of moving the foursome along to the boat before dark. She purposely changed her path when she saw Hank headed for the dock and entered the office from the back door.

"Oh, no," Cindy said. "It's Ranger Rick and the whale patrol. What did you do, Rick, tell these folks that the Park is now closed to all sightseeing?"

"He recommends we don't patronize your Humpback Island resort," Cliffy said. He says you're all trespassing."

"I wouldn't listen to this federal jerk," Cindy replied. "Come on. Let's go before we all get busted for stepping on the wrong rock or something. The cook's got a wonderful fresh fish dinner waiting for you."

Cindy turned and walked out the door. Penny hurried after her, relieved to leave the discussion behind. The other three visitors followed.

"Okay, Cindy, what's this all about?" Penny asked.

"Sounds to me like this island is the source of an interesting squabble, not to mention some obvious opinions on your part."

"It's just all nuts!" Cindy said, with a note of pain in her voice. "You don't want to know. Everybody and their cousin wants to steal Humpback Island from everybody else. And I live there. You're probably one of them. I suppose you belong to some society or another who thinks they should kick everybody off the island."

"Not really," Penny said. "Cliffy and Jessica are kind of interested in the outcome. But I'm not. I just came along for the ride."

Cindy tried to shift the conversation. "If we don't get a move on, we'll miss dinner," she said. Changing her stride, Cindy tried to move ahead of Penny.

"Now wait a minute. You're about the coldest hostess I've ever encountered. I think you owe us an explanation," Penny said, while trying to catch up. Cindy laughed, "As I said, I live on Humpback Island, and if it was up to your Cliffy, the ranger, the old guy Hank who I passed on the path, or anybody else, you'd all kick me off that island—my home, damn it—so you could have a private playground," Cindy replied. "We don't own it, but we don't abuse it or stop anybody else from enjoying it. We just don't want one group or the other to lock it up."

"Huh. Maybe I can help," Penny said.

"What do you mean you're not interested?" Cindy asked. "I told you everybody and their uncle wants a piece of that island, and you would've come 'along for the ride' if you weren't somehow tied up with it."

"No, you said everybody and their cousin," Penny argued. "I would like to see some fairness come out of this now that I've heard a little."

"Oh, great Gawd! That's all we need—more fingers in the pie," Cindy exclaimed.

"We'll see," Penny huffed and ended it for now.

The boat ride to Humpback was silent. The visitors had not anticipated anything so spectacular. The Fairweather Mountains protruded above Glacier Bay in sparkling grandeur. A pod of killer whales were feeding near Point Gustavus. By the island, humpback whales breached all around the boat. Jessica pulled out her cameras and clicked frantically. Cliff forgot all about the fax machine. Gary noticed the jumping salmon and pawed the fishing rods. He asked to stop and give it a try. Cindy ignored them all.

"This place is unreal!" Penny exclaimed. A whale breached close to the boat. "I can't believe it.

This is paradise." She had a permanent smile locked onto her face.

Cindy forgot her resistance to her guests. She was also in her own paradise. On days like this she remembered why she lived here and why she liked to share it with visitors.

When the boat idled to the small pier built by the captain's crew from San Diego, something was awry. Weird John's green-and-brown camouflage skiff was afloat loose off the pier's west tie-down. Captain San Diego sat on the deck boards with a wet rag held tight to his jaw. Tad's troller was tied up while Tad stood over the captain, hands on hips, shaking his head. He caught Cindy's lines.

"What's up?" Cindy asked.

"Oh, boy," Tad groaned, and shook his head again.

Captain San Diego continued his discernment of the deck boards. "I'll be a son of a bitch," he moaned over and over again.

"No, really," Cindy said as she tied the cruiser to the aft cleat. "Shouldn't somebody try to catch Weird John's skiff before it drifts away?"

"I suppose—guess so," Tad replied. He made no motion to do so, however.

"Come on, Tad, what in the hell is going on here?" Cindy asked again. Cliffy jumped over the rail to the deck.

"Ah, well, the Captain, here, and Weird John had a bit of an argument," Tad explained. "I better get the commando skiff." Tad jumped aboard his own skiff tied alongside his troller. Cliff pushed him away. Within a moment, Tad had both skiffs tied to the pier.

Cliff kneeled before the fallen man on deck. "Captain! My God, I didn't know it was you," he exclaimed. "What the hell are you doing?"

"Oh damn…got coldcocked by a wild man," the Captain answered. Dazed, he held onto the rag on his jaw.

Tad stepped forward. He turned to Cindy and said, "The captain, here, and Weird John got into fisticuffs because the Captain was moving the commando skiff to make room for your cruiser. The captain's had one too many martinis and Weird John, you know, is as high as a kite."

"Where's John?" Cindy asked.

The Captain came alive. "He swore he'd come back and untie my boats if I ever did it again," he said. "Here," he reached for Cliffy, "help me up. We've got to get you guys up to the lodge before the shootin' begins."

Jessica and Penny overheard Tad and the Captain. Jessica stood by the pilothouse door in shock, mouth open, hovering. Penny flew into action. "C'mon," she beckoned, glaring at Gary, who toyed with the fishfinder, "do what he says. Help with the gear."

A heavy clamor of footsteps echoed on the pier ramp. "Okay, asshole, you asked for it," Weird John growled. *Boom, boom!*

Everybody dived for the deck. "Holy mother of God!" Cliffy screamed as he lurched into the water. A spray of lead careened three-sixty over their heads and kicked up sand on the beach side.

"Okay, Captain S. In the future, don't mess with my skiff," the gunman screamed. Weird John turned to disappear over the island horizon.

"I liked it," Gary whispered, peering over the boat gunnel. "I'll use it in the next episode of…"

"Shut up, dummy," Jessica demanded. "We could have

died. They were real bullets." Gary didn't reply.

"Everybody," Cindy announced, "I think the coast is clear. He won't be back. He was just blowing off steam. He fired the shotgun away from any harmful directions—like us. Let's get the gear up to the lodge and have dinner."

"I need a drink," Cliffy proclaimed.

"Me, too," Captain S. agreed. "I'll buy."

"Yeah, I could use a beer," Tad added.

Despite the unique welcome, when the four guests were ready to leave Humpback Island, they were more relaxed than they could remember. Gary caught more fish than he could ever dream of. He promised to bring the whole crew back after his next film. Cindy talked him into releasing those that were barely hooked. He couldn't believe it when he actually let her set free a 100 pound halibut. "You've got to be kidding," he moaned.

Jessica ran out of film on the third day. She was content to walk the beaches with no camera on the fourth day, and by the time she left, a little mud or sand on her clothes felt good. One day she ran into Weird John on one of the island's more remote beaches and the two somehow ironed out the shooting incident. "I never liked that son of a bitch," John grunted. "A little scare now and again will keep him from taking over the whole island."

One thing led to another, and the two fell madly into each other's arms. Ol' Gus was on a beach debris excursion and caught them in an embarrassing embrace. It was no secret when Jessica boarded the plane in Gustavus with one of Weird John's camouflage shirts tied around her waist. Jessica told Penny, "A little fling with a real man every now and again keeps me grounded. We're meeting in Mexico this fall."

Cliffy and Captain San Diego stayed up into the wee hours each night, sipping brandy by a beach fire and telling stories of their world travels. They had known each other for several years, having met on a cruise in Mexico. The politics of Humpback Island entered their conversations and Cliffy agreed to see what he could do to prevent the Captain from being evicted.

Penny and Cindy became friends. Cindy introduced Penny to the Humpback's people: Ol' Gus, Aunt Bess, Jimmie, Wilbur, Debbie and her kids and chickens. And, of course, she met Frank. Penny let Cindy know she was jealous of her life, especially her relationship with Frank.

"You keep your hands off him," Cindy said, kidding.

"No problem. But you better not let him loose from your secret leash, Cindy," Penny teased. "I've never known a man so laid back, so comfortable."

"Guess I'm pretty lucky," Cindy said.

When Penny returned to Washington, D.C., she and Cliffy filed for non-profit corporate status of a new organization. She wrote an article for the "Post" about it. "The National Unprotected, Unspecified, and Unowned Territory Society" or "N.U.U.U.T.S.," it was named.

"Humpback Island is a unique experiment," Cindy was quoted in her article: "A chance to see what happens when nobody has more power than another; where a group of people have set out to manage their lives and their environment without government and special interest intervention."

Penny remembered vividly what Cindy said that first day on their way to the boat. "It's just all *nuts*," Cindy had said. "Everybody and their cousin wants to steal Humpback Island from everybody else."

When the Court heard all the arguments of all the prospective owners of Humpback Island, the judge liked Cindy's testimony the best. "What right does anyone have to prevent everybody else from enjoying this paradise, this natural wonder?" she asked. "Even the National Park Service has become a narrow-minded special interest group of its own. We recommend that the Court throw the whole matter out and allow Humpback Island to carry on without rules and laws and ownerships and restrictions and 'no trespassing' signs. Maybe there ought to be just one little place on this earth that is a little bit like heaven."

On that, the Court tabled the matter...indefinitely. The only action taken by the judge was to officially name Humpback Island an "Unspecified Territory" of the United States.

Cindy has said "No, not of the United States! Humpback Island is an unspecified territory of the *planet!* And yes, it is a little like heaven. And even then, it could be a bit better."

Chapter 17

Independence Day

THERE IS ONE DAY OF THE YEAR FOR HUMPBACK Islanders when all stops are pulled for defining those who land here or stay here for any length of time can never forget their experience. It is an almost religious spectacle of downright rebellious freedom that comes from the hardship, isolation and reliance of living without roads, cable T.V., K-Mart, and people you don't know. The islanders broadcast on this day that they're different, they're tough, they're weird, they know how to have fun without a whole bunch of money, and in spite of little differences of opinion now and again, they wouldn't trade their life here for anything else. The Fourth of July is truly an independence day; the number one celebration of life.

Every year a week or two before the Fourth, some mysterious person hangs a list of events on the post office wall. The idea is, of course, that everyone in the community will sign up to sponsor at least one "Fourth" event, such as the annual horseshoe tournament or egg toss. Not everyone signs up. Year after year the same people put on pretty much the same events. What's more, these same people are expected to run these events pretty much the same way every year no matter what their situation or the weather might be.

For instance, last year was the eighth year that dear Aunt Bess sponsored the horseshoe tournament. She had taken first prize each Fourth for all eight years so "Why not? It only makes sense," other potential contenders said. Folks got so tired of the same outcome that they left her in charge in hopes it might shake her winning streak. It hasn't worked yet.

Four years ago while in practice for the big event, her well-used bones just gave out, and her right pitching arm separated from her shoulder on a permanent sort of basis.

Not to be outdone, she started right in practicing with her left arm. By the morning of the big day she was not yet in perfect pitching tune. Being in charge, she changed the tournament to be doubles only. It was no big surprise that her partner was the second best shoe pitcher on the island and thirty-six years her junior. Wilbur had come very close to licking her in years past. Now he was unbeatable, thanks to his elder teammate.

Only on the day of the Fourth of July, do the islanders fondly refer to this seventy-six-year-old neighbor as "Stretch Bess" or "Aunt Bestes Leftus." The winning streak continues.

The annual egg toss is one of the many Fourth events that everybody anticipates. The best guess as to exactly why that is...well, it's the thrill of tossing such a messy projectile with wanton abandon, free to be juvenile no matter what your age. The bigger the splat, the greater the thrill. No doubt some of the thrill comes from throwing something that takes an awful lot of chicken fuss to make and creates a terrible mess when it collides with one's skull.

Humpback Island's chief chicken handler is a feisty young lady named Debbie. She ships a boatload of chicken feed up from Seattle and spends all year cleaning the mess and gathering the eggs. She feeds her three daughters plenty of eggs and sells the leftovers for gas money to fuel her 1974 Ford pickup. When the old blue Ford backs up to the island picnic site loaded with a month or two of her prize eggs, it's time for the egg toss. Debbie's kids each grab an armload of used cartons of eggs and everybody on the island lines up for the annual contest.

Debbie's mom, Delia, "the egg toss queen," and her young camouflage friend, Weird John, have never lost a toss. Her trick is an obvious one: Wait till everybody else has smashed their egg on their partner and then make one toss. Of course, it always breaks but it's the last toss. Year after year, nobody remembers Delia's trick until all the eggs are splattered but one—hers. Some say that the egg is the same as last years and it's hard boiled.

The most popular event of the day results when a fool slides down a Crisco-covered lodge pole pine supplied by Ol' Gus. It used to be that Ol' Gus had a lot of timber on his acreage in Gustavus. But over the years he logged off or sold every stick. So now somebody tows a barked pole from the mainland and Gus pretends it's his. Gus supplies the can of Crisco. He always declares, "That was my straightest pine." He shakes his head in a mock lament for the perfect tree, cuts a slit in the skinniest end, wedges a dollar in it, and then leans the greasy thing over the saltwater slough. The object is to slide down the pole in such a way that you can grab the dollar before splashing into the slough.

Gus has never tried the trick. He's always said, "Anybody who'll try this is a darned fool." But there's a standing rumor around that Gus will try it if Stretch Bess will put a thousand dollar bill on the end. The rumored reply from Bess lingers year to year that she'll put up the "grand" if Ol' Gus beats her at a round of shoes. Reportedly Gus always replies, "If I beat you at a round of shoes, then you'll have to skinny down that pole." All bets remain at an expected stalemate.

After the luscious potluck, complete with fresh-caught Halibut, beach asparagus and fiddlehead salads, pickled kelp, homegrown potatoes, and wild strawberry pie, the band sets up for the evening dance. The fun part over the years has been to guess which band members were currently cohabitating. Something about playing in the island string band—romance partners kept switching, and one never knew who was going to wink at whom, let alone which instrument would start the lick. The fiddle player and the caller were married last year. The year before, the caller was sleeping with the banjo player, and so on. Since the group only performs for an audience twice a year, for the Fourth and for Halloween, it takes awhile to get the songs going. But once the right wink hits the current partner, the tunes get flying and it doesn't matter who winks at whom.

Stretch Bess grabs Ol' Gus; egg queen Debbie forgets who's who and takes the hand of her second husband, the first husband of the caller; Weird John, stoned out of his mind, picks his egg toss mate, Delia, and within seconds the whole island is jumping to the Virginia reel. Exhaustion from the three-leg race, the cake walk, the tug-of-war, the greased pole, and the chainsaw throw stops no one. Until the twilight of the Alaskan summer midnight beckons everyone to a homemade fireworks display by none other than Weird John, independence is do-si-doed right down to the island's wildflower roots.

One by one the island's tired inhabitants snake their way from the picnic grounds to the water's edge. Weird John, now totally paranoid and slit-eyed, has saved enough gun powder and illegally mailed Chinese packages to set the beach sand on fire. At exactly midnight military time John ignites his composition. The children scream for delight while their parents run for cover.

Weird John's sense of direction left him years ago. Last year a misguided rocket with a loud report at its brilliant finale rendered Debbie's chickens permanently deaf. Poor cacklers thought the feed bag had become automated. The year before that, he set the dump afire. No problem though, everyone on the island is a volunteer fireman and most every one of them are ready and waiting on the fireworks beach.

The island's children scurry about the sand lighted by the sparks and the red midnight sunset. Parents and grandparents, young lovers and amazed tourists celebrate the incredible sight— absurd and surreal, unbelievably pure. It's as if everyone is chanting, "We have made it through one more year, one more winter. We are tough. We are truly free."

Chapter 18

Sunsets

THE DAY AWAKENED COLD FOR JUNE. AT PRECISELY
three-fifteen in the morning, the sun crested the Chilkat Mountains. A late frost sparkled on the new grasses and birds per-
formed a symphony. Aunt Bess heard the music and pulled out
of bed early for a walk.

It had been her custom on the fair-weather walks to visit
the cows first, to pet their noses. The mother cow, named October by a vote of the school children, munched on green grass
and basked in the early warmth. May, the first offspring of
October, scratched herself on a post. She had given October a
grandson just a little over a month before. The school kids voted
to name him Spring. Cute as a bull can be, Spring still slept in
the bed May had formed with her body.

"Good morning, ladies," Bess greeted. "What a wonderful
morning we have." She petted the nose of the eager October.
May excused herself from the post and clumped over for her
turn of the lady's attention. Teats jiggled heavy with milk. "My,
my, you have a load there, young lady," Bess remarked.

Bess gave them both her customary attention and excited
utterings, then moved on. "Have a nice day ladies. Ha, ha."
She chuckled at the little Spring all curled up in the frosty grass.
She made her way over to the small shed erected as a milking
room. The duty roster listed Darlene responsible for today's
chores. Darlene and her two children would get the milk and share
any extra with the eighth person above her name on the list.

"Oh, oh," Bess mumbled with a bent smile. Darlene didn't

care much for Weird John. Bess could hear Darlene complain, "Damn lazy bum. It's no excuse to be a Veteran. All he ever does is smoke dope and mooch cigarettes. There's plenty of work around here. He ought to get a job."

Bess sort of agreed with Darlene but enjoyed Weird John's long speeches about the evils of capitalism. Darlene had lost a house to fire, a husband to the sea, and a baby to crib death. For her, no war trauma could win the disaster contest. Bess, herself, had served in the Philippines as a nurse during World War II, had seen two husbands die of cancer, and her son die of an auto accident. But now she was old enough to accept all kinds of people.

Bess, forever amused with the cows, the people, the Island and all the things they shared together, passed the firehall and the school and then turned down to the little dock. Charter operators arrived to prepare their boats for the day's customers. Norm bustled on his boat, as did Frank and Jimmie on their salmon trollers. A very large cruiser idled, one of the lodge fleet. A young blond man, cigarette hanging from his lips, unloaded bait from the on-board freezer for today's hooks.

Aunt Bess continued her journey down the beach toward the mouth of Humpy Creek, her destination. She wanted to see what birds cavorted there today in this bright sunshine. The frost melted beneath her feet. She smiled, proud of herself for covering her garden the evening before with clear plastic to protect it from the killing frost. Others would have to replant for the shortened season.

Ahead at the mouth of the creek she spotted a lone figure squatting on a log. "Darn," she exclaimed. "Wouldn't you know." She wanted to be the first to come upon the spot. As she neared the log, Bess recognized the floppy handmade wool hat. "Gus." Her mood brightened. They had run into each other here before.

"Hi, you old coot," Bess greeted.

Gus jumped almost a foot off the log. "Good golly, young lady. Ya' jump-started my pumper."

"Sorry," Bess replied. "Fancy meeting you here. Out of bed pretty darned early to beat me."

"Didn't sleep much. I couldn't wait for the morning after seeing the clear night," Gus explained.

"Sit. Some baby geese up ahead." He patted the log.

"They're goslings," Bess corrected. She wiped dry a flat surface with her hanky.

"By golly, this is nice," Gus declared. "I haven't broke loose to do the sun-up in years. Usually I'm wrestlin' about fixing something by now. Ya' might get a sunburn today, young lady."

Bess winked. She loved how Gus always flattered her with the title "young lady." Everybody else either called her Aunt Bess or "Stretch" for her six-foot frame and her unbeatable horseshoe form.

They watched in silence. Bess appraised Gus more than the creek or the birds. Six or seven years ago the island celebrated Ol' Gus's eightieth birthday. She guessed he was her senior by a ten or so. Today he didn't appear as pert as usual; maybe a little pale or simply disheveled from his sleepless night. He had been such a good-looking man. Still was. Unevenly shaved gray and white bristles shone in the bright light. A drop of dew hung from his nose hairs. She noticed his left hand and arm shook with a slight palsy. He appeared to be on the verge of tears, and she too began to cry—a silent cry so he wouldn't notice. She had no clear idea why.

Bess's vision blurred. She remembered back to the first time she saw Gus, not Ol' Gus, but forty years ago when his lovely wife Edith was alive. He and Edith had maneuvered his fishing boat to haul a load of logs up the Goode River. Bess hunted berries on the bank. Gus was tall and square-shouldered, lean, as appealing as a man could be. Quiet, he always smiled, even when he was angry or scolding a son or a neighbor. The bushy dark eyebrows strutted forward from his brow as if they signaled his deep understanding of life, of love. He could have been a movie star or a president. For sure, he modeled the real goods that movies were made from, the man a president yearned to appear to be.

"See that hump on Pleasant?" Gus asked. "Have you ever been on top?"

Bess stirred from her bleary dreaming. "No...why, no, I haven't," she replied, clearing her voice. Her skin tingled, as if she had nestled next to a handsome young man on a first date.

"The Natives say the hump is magic," Gus said. "I believe it is. Maybe someday I'd like to live up there."

Bess couldn't think of anything to say. Another tear erupted from deep within to flow to the edge of her eye. She dabbed at her moist cheek, and the movement of her arm seemed to startle them, the geese stirred. *Cackle—Honk.* All at once they took flight in resounding rhythm of large wings. Ducks and seagulls startled from the goose thunder.

The old couple watched as if amazed by every bird, every move.

When the geese had gone and the other birds had settled back by the creek to eat and splash in the glorious morning sun, Gus stood suddenly. "Got to get to work," he mumbled.

Bess noticed Gus creak his joints and maneuver his old muscles. No, he didn't look well, she thought. He had never looked so old to her. Then he glanced back at her and she shied away, embarrassed to be staring.

"I'll meet you here tonight, okay?" Gus asked.

"It'll be a grand sunset." He shuffled his wool cap to sit back on his head. "Okay, at sunset, young lady," he answered himself and confirmed her silent reply at the same time.

Bess stood slowly too. Her back ached from the position she had fashioned on the log. "Yep, guess I should get to the garden and rescue the plants before the plastic cooks 'em," Beth said. "Yes, kind sir, I most certainly will meet you tonight."

They both turned and walked back towards the dock.

"Thank you, Gus, for a wonderful morning," Bess said.

Gus took Bess's hand. He stopped to get a good gentle grip, looked her intensely in the eye and said, "By golly, young lady, you're very welcome. The pleasure was mine." The two strolled to the dock, hand in hand. The sun became brilliant behind them. Morning dew clung to their high top rubber boots.

Bess mused about the coming evening throughout the day while she toiled and played in her perfect garden. Mostly flowers these days, although in past years the garden provided potatoes, carrots, onions and greens for much of the year's food needs. Her interest had become the brilliant colors, the sweet smells. She transplanted flowers each spring all over the island. The neighbors were confounded with her energy, in awe of her superb taste and skill.

When the evening came and the sun took its dip into the northwest, Bess cleaned herself up and, of all things, put on a touch of perfume and a dab of rouge. Maybe it wasn't a real date, but it was the closest thing to it she'd had in thirty years.

Again she stopped to pet the cows. This time, October was sleeping. Spring and May romped in the evening sun. They came quickly to her call and eagerly jutted their noses for Bess's usual rub.

Further down the trail, she stooped to pick some early wildflowers and held them carefully in her hand, lifting them occasionally to smell the sweet aroma.

At the creek, she threw a stone in a pool and remembered the hours she had tossed rocks years ago with her son. Now, one stone was enough. The pain of arthritis reminded her of her age.

Gus was not in sight.

She sat still for awhile on the log waiting, watching the birds come into the calm tidepools at the mouth. Time passed quickly with the birds' incessant cackles and squawks, the sweet smell of the night coming on. Hundreds of birds gathered. Geese nestled on the grasses above the tideline. Ducks settled into the shallow pools. Shorebirds bustled.

A red blush spilled over the mountains to the east. She turned back away from the creek and looked to the northwest. The sun dipped behind the Fairweather Mountains. It had somehow gotten late. Where was Gus?

The sunset glowed orange and red, half above the ice-blue mountains. Thin clouds on the horizon tinted the colors to make a rainbow of the entire planet.

Bess remembered Gus's dream to someday live on the Pleasant Island hump. She turned to the south to see the hump glow blue and red. It was eerie. She shivered. Suddenly every bird jumped in a clamor of cackles, honks, and piercing squeals. The feathered cloud lifted in unison. Bess trembled in awe of the sight. She could think of no reason for the sudden ruckus.

Swirling circles, wings flapping in a chorus, a strange mix of birds fluttered and turned in the direction of Gus's magic hump, a good five miles from her position. As if they evaporated, the birds disappeared from Bess's vision directly into the top of the Native's mysterious place.

When sun sank below and behind the snow-capped mountains to the north, a pale orange glow remained. Shaken from the sight of the birds and the incredible radiance of the sunset moments before, Bess stood up. Her skin tingled like it had with Gus at her side earlier that morning. Come to think of it, her skin had tingled ever since she had arrived at the creek. "Oh, my," she exhaled with a sigh. She trembled with the thought. Ol' Gus had promised, "At sunset, young lady."

Bess ambled very slowly back up the beach, wanting to see a late Gus hurrying to make his date. But she knew better. A sad smile stuck on her face all the way to her cabin. And tears wetted her red cheeks. She would miss her old friend.

Ol' Gus's three children and eight grandchildren came to the island over the next two or three days. Aunt Bess made sure they knew of his wishes—his next "someday" home. When it came time to scatter the ashes, Bess volunteered to lead the way to the mystical rise, the hump on Pleasant Island. The site was truly wonderful, "magic," so Gus had said. She felt the goosebumps when the small urn was uncapped by Gus's eldest son.

"Oh God I'm lucky. He was such a fine friend," Bess proclaimed. Bess let loose her contagious laughter. Tears of joy ran down her cheeks and she reveled in the magic of Gus's new-found home.

Epilogue

A VIOLENT STORM CAUGHT US OFF GUARD. THE TINY boat tossed with the breaking seas. Both fishing rods out in their holders trailed a line, a weight, a flasher and a herring. I tried my best to keep the boat straight against the incoming waves and had to juice the throttle. The flasher and herring bounced uselessly on the surface of each curling breaker.

Little Emmy watched behind while I concentrated on the crashing bow. "Dad, Dad," she hollered, "there's a giant fish on my line."

"Don't worry, honey. We'll be up the river and safe soon," I shouted over the noise of the engine and the thrashing waves.

"No, Dad, there's a whale or something back there," Emmy insisted.

I turned in time to see a large hump dive beneath the last wave; her pole holder and rod snapped from the gunnel and flew overboard. Oh, my God, she was right. We had hooked a whale.

"Dad, Dad, the pole's broke, the pole's broke."

The whole scene became a frustrating haze of waves and whales. Flashes of bright daylight interfered with the gray storm. Her green-colored rain slicker became an unclear fuzz with a green nightie.

"Dad, Dad, my bowl's broke. Wake up, Dad. The earthquake broke my bowl."

I forced myself to catch one picture or another. "Don't worry, honey, we'll be up the river, safe, in a few minutes," I mumbled.

"Dad, Dad..." she said again as she tugged at my arm. "What river?"

I struggled to the odd sight of sunlight, open curtains, wrinkled covers. "Oh," I moaned.

Later that morning, on our way to the beach dump, we passed our neighbor, Dan, astride his backhoe. "Where are you running to today?" I asked for the sake of friendly conversation.

"Haven't you heard?" Dan replied. "Hank has blocked the beach at the dock. We're having an old fashioned protest."

"Why in the hell did he do that?" I asked.

"He thinks he owns the beach and put up a damned chain."

I pulled ahead of Dan; we were blocking the narrow road. A chain of cars and trucks passed us on the way to the dock.

When we arrived at the scene of the community protest, Emmy so clearly asked the pertinent question, "Why did he do that, Dad? Nobody owns the beach."

"Ha!" I bellowed. A wee tear rose from the bottom of my soul to flavor the laughter.